Light
THE
Heart Home

CONNOR FALLS CHRISTMAS SERIES
NOVELLA

Robin Maderich

POTTER STREET BOOKS
ZIONSVILLE PA
2024

© 2022 Robin Maderich
All rights reserved.

ISBN: 979-8-9914596-5-5

Printed in the U.S.A.

Cover design by Robin Maderich

Potter Street Books/Robin Maderich Publishing
www.potterstreetbooks.com

This book is also available in digital format.

Light

THE

Heart Home

"Family is not
an important thing.
It is everything."
— **Michael J. Fox**

AUTHOR'S NOTE

Light the Heart Home is the second novella from the Connor Falls Christmas Collection. I have wanted to make each story in that collection into its own special edition in celebration of family, love, life, and Christmas, and now I have. Find a warm, comfy spot and enjoy!

Merry Christmas everyone.

Yours,

Robin Maderich

Chapter One

Emma flipped the car visor down, squinting into the sun. Driving due west on a winter's afternoon presented its problems. It didn't help that the defroster had decided to malfunction several hours into the trip's second leg. Every ten minutes or so while warm air chugged feebly on full blast through all vents, she'd been wiping the windshield with an old towel she'd found in the trunk. Thank goodness for gloves and a heated seat.

For the first time in more years than she cared to count, Emma was going home for Christmas. She'd had no particular reason to return before. Connor Falls had stopped being her home when the last Parsons sibling left it. What was there to go home to, if all the family had gone? Most Connor Falls' families had some member, or even multiple members, living in or near the small town their whole lives, but after Mom and Dad decided to retire and move south, Emma, her two sisters and her brother had headed elsewhere, one by one.

Emma couldn't imagine what whim had drawn her little sister to return to Connor Falls. Not only to live, but to start a business, making and selling candles and soaps and lotions, of all things. Sophie had rented a little storefront on a side street and set up shop, a move Emma would not have expected from the girl who'd gone to school for business and graphic design. Despite Sophie's free spirit tendencies, she'd always been sensible. She'd been the one who'd led the parade to get the heck out of Dodge, finding a job right after school that had made their parents proud. Emma had been sure Sophie would never look back.

A sigh escaped Emma's lips, fogging glass. Snapping up the towel, she wiped the condensation away. When she threw the rag back onto the seat, it struck her sister's postcard, the one Sophie had sent following their phone call two weeks ago. Emma picked it up, glancing from the glossy card to the traffic ahead and back again.

Sophie's Chandlery: Light the Heart Home.

The photo was nice—a single crimson pillar candle off-center in a frosted windowpane—but the store's name, the sentiment, seemed a bit pretentious. Emma tossed the card into the cubbyhole beneath the radio. She would need it for the address once she got into town.

Of all her siblings, Emma had possessed the strongest reason to leave Connor Falls, and that reason still existed. She didn't talk about what had happened much, even with her friends. She was supposed to be over it, given time's passage. She did speak to Sophie about old feelings on occasion, a fact which made it all the more strange to find her sister using the one carrot to lure Emma's return to Connor Falls that Sophie knew she wouldn't be able to resist.

Sophie had a secret.

Despite all Emma's speculation and prodding, Sophie refused to spill on the phone. She didn't want anyone else to know either. Not yet. She had made Emma promise not to even mention the possibility of news. As if. Emma didn't go calling family members to gossip, or even to check up on them. Not often, anyway. They usually ended up calling her when sufficient time had passed to warrant a conversation. They all joked about how much Emma hated the phone.

And yet she kept her cell glued to her side at all times. Work, she always told herself. Only she didn't have that excuse anymore.

Emma reached into the car door pocket and pulled out the water bottle she'd been swigging from for the past three hours. She drank sparingly, chill liquid running down her throat. With a glance in the mirror before changing lanes, Emma spotted the cardboard boxes filling her back seat. More crammed the trunk. Her printer and laptop were belted in on the passenger seat beside her. Winter boots, in case she needed them in a hurry, lay on the floor beneath the glove box alongside a backpack filled with her immediate needs.

Emma had her own secret, one that would never have led her back to Connor Falls if she could have helped it. But then Sophie had called.

This was going to be some Christmas.

*   *   *

Sophie flicked the forest-green linen napkin down over a wooden crate centered in the shop window. She admired the contrast between aged wood and crisp fabric. She wondered if this was what the designers called 'shabby-chic'. Didn't matter what it was called, really. She liked the appearance. That was good enough for her.

Two holly sprigs were angled at the crate's outer edges. A cranberry-red pillar candle stood between them slightly off center in a faux, glassless window pane, mimicking the postcard she had designed for use with the promotional holiday giveaway. Fake snow had been sprinkled over the display. Beside the candle a small placard read: NEWLY SPRUNG FROM THE MOLDS TO GRACE YOUR TABLE – NINE-INCH TALL SOY AND BEESWAX PILLARS.

Emma had called an hour ago explaining some ongoing malfunction with her car, a need for gas and a pit stop, but that she'd be arriving soon. Sophie had a major secret she planned to share with Emma. She might have considered doing it over the phone, if Emma hadn't sounded so down in the dumps. Emma needed to be with family, even if only her sister.

Glancing up, Sophie noticed a dark-haired woman at the window, partially silhouetted by the streetlamp behind. She appeared to be studying the elements in the display with a perplexed wrinkle on her brow. Sophie's heart gave a jolt. She ran to the door and threw it open.

"Emma!"

Hunched against the cold in a gray woolen knee-length coat, Emma turned and hesitated, her perpetually bitten lower lip tight in a toothy grasp. Nothing ever changed. Emma, the never-impetuous, couldn't even work up the spontaneity to hug Sophie first. Sophie had no such issues. Charging along the sidewalk, arms outstretched, she tossed herself at her sister, forcing Emma to wrap her arms around Sophie or risk them toppling together onto the ground.

After a few breathless exclamations, Emma pulled away first. "You look…remarkable," she said, eyeing Sophie up and down. Sophie noted her gaze lingered on certain salient points, such as what Emma no doubt viewed her rather plain dress and the hair she'd let grow out. Sophie wore it now in a manner that couldn't help but inspire Emma's disapproval, but it hadn't been intentional. Lastly, Emma's gaze stuck on the necklace at Sophie's throat. Emma nodded at the jewelry. "Not one of my designs."

"Sis," said Sophie with a laugh, "I can't afford one of your designs."

Emma snorted. "At this point in time, I can't afford one of mine, either."

Sophie laughed again, ending it a little uncertainly. Since when had Emma gone so deadpan? Or wasn't it a joke? In a moment, however, Emma's mouth curved in her crooked, signature smile. Emma was a beauty and always had been. Mismatched brows, a slight bump on her nose from a fly ball, the irregular smile, didn't detract but added up to something truly special. All the boys in high school had been quite aware of Emma. Sophie by comparison was the pixie sister. They said so charmingly, but Sophie read between the lines. In time, she'd made her own way among them, but for a long while the difference had been quite irksome.

"How was the ride?" Sophie asked her.

"Long," said Emma, mouth still curved, yet the smile didn't reach her eyes.

"Ems, are you okay?"

"I'm fine. Just a bit tired."

Sophie tipped her head and looked around her sister's arm to the street. "Where'd you park?"

Emma jerked her thumb over her shoulder. "Around the block. It was the only spot."

"There's one right there," Sophie pointed out.

"There wasn't when I drove past the first time."

Sophie flinched at her sister's tone. Definitely not fine.

Tucking her hand into Emma's elbow, Sophie steered her toward the shop door. "Love your coat. And your boots. You're still Elegant Emma."

Emma shrugged. "Thanks…I guess. You'd think I'd have changed a bit in a year and a half."

"It hasn't been that long!"

"Oh yes," said Emma, "it has."

"Yikes," Sophie muttered, yanking open the door and releasing the scents from within. Beside her, Emma jerked to a halt, brown eyes widening. Her nose wrinkled a little as she sniffed. Another smile played about her lips, more relaxed, maybe more authentic.

"Soph," Emma whispered, "I…I never would have pictured you doing this. What on earth has happened to you?"

Funny, Sophie had been about to ask Emma the same thing.

*   *   *

Inside the shop, Emma shirked her coat grudgingly from her shoulders. She didn't want to give the garment up. The last hour in the car had chilled her to the bone. She wondered if Billy Stiles was still around. He'd always been good with a car. He'd probably taken over his father's shop like his dad always wanted.

Emma cut her thoughts short, amazed at how quickly they had reverted to people and memories from the past. What was the point? Her life wasn't here.

She would have to get her car fixed, though. She'd look for someone on-line in the next couple days.

"What?" she said, noticing Sophie had come to stand at her side, hand out.

"Your coat," Sophie said, as if she'd said it already, which she probably had. "I'll hang it up. Unless you'd rather go straight upstairs? I have to finish a few things down here."

Emma stuffed her gloves into her pocket before handing her sister the coat. "Upstairs? Is that where you're living?"

"Yep, didn't I say? I'm sure I must have. I live in

the apartment above. Quite convenient, really. The commute is all of about thirty seconds." Sophie hung Emma's garment on an old coat rack painted over in black enamel, the spiral elements on the wood embellished in lavender, pink and turquoise. Emma spied a cardstock tag hanging from an arm by a silver ribbon. The store logo was recognizable on the tag and what would probably prove upon closer inspection to be the price.

"Your handiwork?" Emma asked.

Sophie took a step back, grinning. "It is," she said. "You like it?"

"Sure," Emma said. "It's different." Emma tucked her hands beneath her arms to warm them.

"Want your gloves back?"

Emma grimaced. "Is it that obvious?"

"A bit. If you'd take a couple of extra steps into the store, you'd find it's quite cozy in here."

Was she hovering by the door? She'd been doing that lately, finding a spot near an exit wherever she went, as if the need might arise for a hasty departure. Well, maybe not the need. More like the desire.

"Sorry," she said.

Sophie waved away her apology, checking her watch. "I put a sign on the door that I was closing early today. Bad form, I know, during the holiday buying season, but I figured you and I could grab a late dinner."

"You don't have to close. I can—"

"The sign's been up all week. Plenty of time for word to get around."

"Okay," said Emma quietly.

"Sit down, Ems. Seriously. You're making me nervous. I have a few things to do and then we can head out. Or will that be too much after your drive?"

"It's fine. It'll be nice." Emma moved to a ladder back chair that had been painted to match the coat rack. The chair, too, held a price tag. Emma avoided looking at the amount as she pointed toward the seat with a questioning glance.

"It's made for sitting," Sophie said. "So sit."

Emma eased herself onto the rattan seat. She clutched her fingers between her knees, gazing around at the store's fragrant contents. There were other furnishings, too, and a rack containing what looked like charmingly illustrated note cards. Emma's gaze finally came to rest on her sister, who appeared to be checking the shelves and making notations on a small pad in her hand. Her outfit, from her dress to her brushed suede boots, looked like something from the nineteen-sixties. Emma supposed that sort of thing was back in style again. Sophie's hair had grown out since the last time Emma had seen her, from shoulder length to long and golden and curly, tamed only by the braids at the front pulled back and fastened behind her head in a hair tie. Perhaps it was some sort of counterculture persona her sister wanted to project, for the sake of the store. On Sophie, however, it looked genuine.

"When did you get all artsy on us, Soph?" she asked.

"I didn't 'get' all artsy," Sophie said, glancing over her shoulder. "I always was."

Emma stood, doing a slow turn to take in the shop again. "Well, you look the part for sure, but I don't remember you being into—" she waved her hands "—this sort of thing."

She hadn't meant the words to sound so dismissive, but the long silence behind her made it clear they'd been exactly that and had wounded Sophie in the process. Shoulders dropping, Emma turned around. "Soph, I'm sorry."

"No," said Sophie. "Don't apologize. I get it. I know where you're coming from. But seriously, this is who I've always been."

"You had a high-paying job in the city," Emma reminded her. "Doing…I don't know exactly what, but something far from this, I'm sure."

Sophie walked behind the counter, brushing her sleeve across three-inch square midnight blue tiles. She smiled down at them. "I made this counter, too, with my own two hands."

"Sophie…"

Her sister looked up. Emma saw it then, in her eyes. A knee-jerk disappointment quickly shuttered.

"What I did at my job in the city, Ems, was design. Artsy stuff, as you call it. And as a kid, I was constantly creating things, painting things, planning things, even experimenting with my old friend Pam making candles. You remember her?"

Sophie didn't wait for Emma to answer, although Emma did, indeed, remember Pam. The two of them, Sophie and Pam, had been quite annoying, really, but now that Sophie mentioned it, they had possessed a certain creativity that seemed to flourish when they were together. Emma had a quick flashback of watching them paint stones one day. Round, flattish stones gathered from the creek bank near the house, later covered in floral designs. Mom and Dad had one on display for the longest time.

"So, yeah, this is who I am," Sophie said. "This is me following my heart totally. Do you think this is beneath me somehow, or is it just that you don't understand it? I know you've always hated when you don't understand something. There isn't much you don't get, Emma, but maybe this is one of those things."

Emma stared at her sister wordlessly.

"There were elements in that job of mine which would have eventually killed the part of me I love," Sophie went on, apparently unable to stop now she'd gotten started. "You have to understand that, surely? You have the creative bug, too. You design the most beautiful jewelry I've ever seen. You know how it feels."

Emma drew short, staggered breaths in through her nose. She didn't want to talk about the jewelry. Not now. She nodded. "I didn't come here to get you all worked up, Sophie. I'm sorry."

"Again," Sophie said with a lift of her fingers, "don't apologize. Take a breath. A deep breath. What do you think?"

Emma did so, filling her lungs. "Well," she

admitted, "I must say, it does smell incredibly lovely in here."

Sophie grinned. Emma's heart pinched.

"But what made you choose candles?" she asked, keeping a careful watch on her sister's eyes.

"Scent, color. I make matching soaps and lotions, too. I know I can't compete with the big stores, but that's why I came back. People here like local. They support local. Did you notice the furniture?"

Emma glanced around at the various pieces decorated in floral patterns, checks, and plaids—sometimes all on the same piece—as well as deliberately primitive animals and landscapes. "It's really something," Emma said. "You have a definite style that comes through."

"As you've probably noticed, all of it's for sale, even the coat rack. So if someone comes in and wants to buy it, you'd better snatch down that expensive coat of yours, pronto."

"I will," said Emma, "unless they want the coat, too. I wouldn't be disinclined to let it go for the right price."

Sophie laughed rather too hard, like a child. Emma observed her in silence, unable to manage an answering amusement.

Chapter Two

Emma attempted to hurry along Main Street. The chill bit at her cheeks and nipped her toes through her soles. She should have changed into the lined snow boots she'd brought. She didn't often need them in her southern existence but had convinced herself that she hadn't gotten so acclimated to the warmer temperatures in Georgia that a little cold would be her undoing. She'd been wrong.

Unfortunately, arm linked through Emma's, Sophie strolled at her side at a snail's pace. Seemed Sophie had decided it was her duty to point out every decorated window from the pub all the way back to Sophie's Chandlery. She had stories to go with most, frequently asking Emma if she remembered this person or that. Emma had stopped answering. She didn't want to remember, didn't want to be drawn into nostalgic reminiscence.

"I don't usually eat this late," Emma said at last, trying for another hint. "I hope I can sleep."

"If I don't grab something while I'm working, I always eat this late," countered her sister drowsily, leaning her head against Emma's shoulder. "And it makes me sleep like a log."

Emma compressed her lips, sucking brittle air in through her nose.

Although the walk back to Sophie's place was becoming increasingly painful, dinner had, at least, been quite pleasant after a delay in leaving the shop. A last minute customer had arrived, rushing through the door five minutes before the altered closing time. Sophie had dealt with the man with more patience than Emma would have displayed. As a result, they'd left for dinner nearly a half hour later than originally intended.

Emma couldn't fault the place they'd eaten—a small tavern that hadn't been there before her departure from Connor Falls—or the conversation during the meal. They'd skirted around any underlying annoyance, as well as the secrets they both held. In Emma's case, she hadn't yet hinted at one. Sophie, for some reason, had decided to make Emma wait on hers. Emma hadn't bothered to try to bring the subject up. Sophie was Sophie. She'd get around to it and probably in a most unexpected manner.

Sophie's head shot upright. "I never actually asked you," she cried.

Given her train of thought, Emma started uncomfortably. "Asked what?"

"If you were staying with me? You are, aren't you? I'd planned it that way, but since I didn't mention, maybe you decided otherwise. You've seen the apartment now. It has plenty of room, even if it's not as big as yours. You'll like it, it's cozy. Please, Ems, stay with me."

Emma patted her sister's hand. "Relax, Sophie. I figured I was." More than figured, Emma had counted on it. She wouldn't say so to Sophie, though. Emma wasn't ready for questions.

"I've got an extra key. Just come and go as you please. You'll probably want to look up old friends while you're here?"

If Sophie had couched that last as a statement rather than a question, Emma likely wouldn't have caught on. Added to the names from their past Sophie had been throwing at her during their walk, Emma suddenly understood. She ceased patting Sophie's fingers and instead removed them from her elbow.

"Sophie, no. I won't be visiting anyone while I'm here but you. There's nothing in my past I want to relive. This isn't old home week for me. Understood?"

Sophie gave a disgruntled nod.

"Honestly, Soph, I don't care about anything I left behind."

"Okay," Sophie said.

"I mean it."

"Okay," Sophie repeated.

"Promise me you won't hound me."

"Okay," Sophie said one more time.

"And don't sulk," added Emma.

Sophie shoved both hands into her coat pockets. "Okay."

Sophie increased her pace. Emma, taller by seven inches, had to hurry to catch up. "You wanted to come back," Emma said breathlessly. "You've pointed out it was right for your business. Great. Maybe you have some fond memories I'm unaware of, but at one point you were as keen as anyone to move on. Yours was the rallying call for exodus, unless I'm mistaken."

Sophie stopped short at the corner. "You're not mistaken, Ems," she said. "But I was."

She turned right and started walking again before Emma could muster a response. "Soph, Soph, slow down," Emma called. At least the faster pace had started to warm her a bit, although her toes remained frozen. Outside the store Sophie halted once more, pivoting to face her, expression not quite readable, eyes glittering. Sophie might have been angry, she might have been hurt, or she might have been just plain cold.

"I was welcomed back," Sophie said, "as a business owner and as someone who had grown up here. And it's not all sentimentality. The side street and smaller store? Cheaper to rent, heat, cool, light than anything I checked into in this area. My tiny apartment—love it, by the way—more affordable by far than the place I had before I came back. The Chandlery inventory? Nothing like it in Connor Falls or anywhere nearby. The changes I made were well thought out, with a good business plan and a good life plan. I wanted roots again, Ems. I have them. I found what I had lost."

Emma released a long breath, frosting the air. Her fingers, unconsciously tightened into fisted knots, uncurled. She pressed her hands against her thighs. "That's good, Soph. I'm so glad for you."

Oddly, Emma wasn't making nice, not merely using words to placate her sister. She meant what she said. A subtle joy on her sister's behalf had sparked in her heart, surprising her like a match in the dark.

"I really am," Emma said.

Sophie's gaze lifted to hers, holding there. A slow smile curled her lips.

"Good. Let's go upstairs and have some hot chocolate."

"Hot chocolate!" Emma gasped, clutching at her middle. "I'm going to barf. How can you still fit anything into that stomach of yours?"

"Easy," said Sophie. "I'm eating for two."

*　　*　　*

That had been rather blunt. Sophie had planned to lead up to it, or at the very least not blurt her news out on the sidewalk. She could almost see the thoughts churning in Emma's head as she sat silently watching Sophie from the kitchen table. Sophie scooped hot chocolate mix into both her mug and Emma's before pouring steaming water from the kettle into each. She held up a bag of marshmallows, shaking it over Emma's mug. Emma shook her head fiercely. "Your loss," said Sophie, dropping two into hers.

No time could be a good time, really. Not for this conversation. But Sophie wanted Emma to be the first in her family to know. There had been a period in their lives when they'd told each other everything.

Sophie carried the hot chocolate to the table, sliding Emma's across to her before sitting down.

"Pregnant," Emma whispered, not as though she'd meant to say the word out loud. She frowned at the steam rising from her cup.

"Yes," Sophie answered, breathing in the sweet scent from her mug. Emma's head jerked up.

"How, Soph? How did this happen?"

Sophie sipped the chocolate, scalding her lip. She quickly put the mug down and pressed her tongue to stinging flesh, wrinkling her nose. "In the usual way," she said, "how else?"

Emma ignored the bright red mug Sophie had placed before her, hands moving like she wanted to shove it away. "This isn't funny."

Sophie had to agree. Not funny at all. Yet all the tears she'd expended in response to the discovery had ended the very next day. Yes, being a single mother wasn't funny, but it also wasn't the end of her world. Not by a long shot.

"Do you…do you have health insurance?"

When had Emma become the one who went straight to practicalities? She hadn't even asked the questions Sophie assumed would be uppermost in her mind, like: Whose is it?

Or: Where is he?

Or: Are you insane?

"I do." When she deemed it safe enough, Sophie took another, tentative sip from her mug. She set the mug down precisely on the damp circle from the chocolate that had dribbled over the edge when she'd burned herself. On the wall behind her head, the kitchen clock she normally never noticed ticked quite loudly in the silence.

"Emma, where's your suitcase?" Sophie asked abruptly. "You're going to need it."

"Not now," said Emma.

Sophie poked a finger at the smeared chocolate on the table. "Are you leaving then? I really didn't think sharing this—this issue with my sister would be a leave-able offense. Now Judy, well, that's a different matter…" Sophie came close to trembling thinking about what would be their older sister Judy's reaction. "It will be difficult to get Judy to understand, but I thought you might. Or at the very least, afford me the comfort of discussing my situation with someone I presumed cared enough about me to want to know."

Goodness, she hadn't meant to say that last bit. It sounded like an attack.

Yep, that was the way Emma had taken it, too. She'd gone very still.

"Emma…"

Emma shook her head in a rapid, barely discernible movement. "I need to think about this."

Sophie reached up and scratched her forehead. With the other hand, she stuck a finger into the mug and lifted out a marshmallow, stuffing it into her mouth whole. "Really?" she mumbled around the warm, melting confection, contorting her face as she tried to subdue and swallow it. "Really?" she repeated when she'd done so. "What is it you need to think about? You're not the one who's pregnant, Ems. I am."

Sophie longed to jump up and yank the battery from the kitchen clock. Picturing the conversation over the past two weeks had never been like this, with the tick-tock of a cheap timepiece punctuating heavy silences.

Emma pushed back her chair and stood. She carried the mug to the sink, poured the cooling chocolate down the drain, rinsed and set the receptacle in the drain board. Turning on her heel she headed for the door, pausing when she reached it, hand on the knob.

"I'll be back," she said in a subdued voice.

Sophie dug once again into her chocolate, searching for the second marshmallow. "Next week? Next year? In a few minutes? I'd like to know if I should be locking the door."

"In a few minutes," Emma said sharply. "I just need to get my stuff from the car."

But she didn't move. Instead, coatless, she stared at the floor. Sophie waited. When Emma didn't speak Sophie stood, too, and went to her.

"Ems?"

Slowly, Emma's head lifted. She looked straight into Sophie's eyes. Sophie recognized the uncertainty, the vague grasping for balance, for hope, in her sister's gaze. It was like looking in a mirror at the woman she, herself, had been.

*   *   *

Emma wasn't a crier. She'd never been a crier. But suddenly she was. A loud one. Through tear-blurred eyes, she watched Sophie scurry across the small apartment and return with a half-empty box of tissues.

"Been using a lot of these lately, have you?" Emma said, snatching out two in order to mop her face and thoroughly blow her nose.

"Shut up, sis," Sophie shot back, eyes glistening, a wavering smile trembling on her lips. "Shut up and sit down."

This time they sat in the living room, which Emma realized belatedly was both cozy and fantastically, eccentrically, artfully decorated. Why hadn't she seen that the moment they walked in? She opened her mouth to compliment her sister now, but Sophie reached out and patted her knee in such a maternal gesture Emma's words stopped dead in her mouth.

Little Sophie was going to be a mom, a single mom, and here Emma sat, bemused and distraught and nigh on hysterical about transformations in her life that were minor by comparison.

Except they weren't. Not really. It was, after all, her life, and she needed to deal with what had happened and what was to come as surely as Sophie.

"Are you going to tell me now?" Sophie asked, leaning forward from the ottoman.

Emma took a deep breath, followed by another. Sophie held out the tissue box again. Emma waved it away with a thank you.

Emma knew Sophie possessed more sense than to believe Emma's hysterics were due to her announcement. Emma wasn't ready to talk, though. Outlining her fall from grace on her first night here hadn't been her plan.

"Emma."

Emma shook her head. "Who's the father?"

Sophie blinked, pulled back. "We're talking about you, now."

"Not yet, Soph. Who is he, if you don't mind telling me?"

Sophie bit her lip. Her eyes rounded. Emma knew that look, remembered that look. Sophie might as well have been ten years old again, and she eleven. The old I-don't-know-if-you're-going-to-like-this face usually rang true.

"Ben," Sophie said.

"Your fiancé?" Shock forced the question from Emma in a harsh croak. "I mean ex-fiancé?"

Sophie nodded. "He called out of the blue three and a half months ago and wanted to try to work things out. He came up for a long weekend. That was all it lasted, but enough time for this." She fluttered a hand over her belly and dropped spread fingers gently onto her abdomen. Her expression softened.

The simple gesture spoke of acceptance, determination, a tender devotion. Seeing it caused the apprehension inside Emma to settle and smooth out, like water when the wind has died down. "Does he know? Ben?"

"Yes," said Sophie. She shook her head.

Emma didn't need to ask anything else. She stood up, pulling Sophie with her.

"Well, let's make this a long story short," Emma said. "I lost my job. Destroyed my job, actually. There's no going back. I wallowed long enough that I could no longer afford my stupidly expensive apartment, so I broke the lease, moved whatever furnishings I couldn't sell together with a few odds and ends into storage, and packed everything else into my car, which is parked around the corner. I really don't know what I'm going to do, but if you don't mind, and you can spare the space, I'd like to bring some of that stuff inside until I figure it out."

*   *   *

Emma snored. Sophie wondered if anyone had ever told her that. Even from the kitchen Sophie could hear the sound, mellow, soft, like an exhausted, sacked-out puppy.

Sophie glanced at the clock that had annoyed her so much earlier in the night. She barely heard it ticking now, but the time displayed by the hands couldn't be ignored. It was after one in the morning.

Yawning, Sophie crossed the living room rug to

the street-facing windows. She sat on the window seat, shoving her feet beneath the folded crocheted blanket. A small wind had arisen after midnight, rattling the panes. In each halo formed by the streetlamps outside snowflakes flew, sparse and delicate, settling on chilled windshields but nowhere else. Emma's car was out there, moved to a space about halfway down the block. Together Sophie and Emma had emptied the front and back seats, piling everything into the tiny bedroom where Emma had curled up on the futon shortly thereafter and fallen asleep.

Sophie's hand strayed as it frequently did to her abdomen. She smiled at the indistinguishable roundness beneath her fingers. "Hey, you," she whispered, breath fogging the glass in front of her face.

Somewhere in there, beneath the slight rolls of easy living and too many fries, a child grew. *Her* child—continuing blood lines, expanding family, bearing traits both familiar and unexpected, throwbacks to a different generation or to ten tiny fingers and toes exactly like her own…or like Ben's.

Her sigh bloomed on the chilled pane. She scrubbed the moisture away with her sleeve, staring out at the swirling flakes sparkling in the lamplight.

The flame on the single candle burning in a hurricane container centered on the sill danced over the glass, reminding Sophie what she'd written long ago when she first contemplated creating Sophie's Chandlery.

Burn one candle in the window, just one flame in the night, and you will light the heart home.

Across the small apartment behind the half-closed door Emma mumbled unintelligibly in her sleep. Sophie smiled.

Life could be strange. Life could be so very strange.

Chapter Three

"I'm not staying past New Year's, Soph. I'm not. I really can't. I have to get my life in order."

For all her effort, Emma's insistence had exited her mouth a bit like a whine. Apparently even Sophie thought so. She clearly struggled against laughing while she flipped Emma's egg in the frying pan.

"And I don't eat eggs," Emma added.

"You could have told me that before I fried it up," Sophie growled. "Anyway," she said, sliding the egg onto a plate next to two buttered slices of toast, "beggars can't be choosers. This is all I've got right now. I didn't make it to the grocery store yesterday."

"Beggars?" Emma retorted as Sophie set the plate before her. "You invited me here."

"I did. And if I give you a list and some cash, will you run to the store for me? Or you could watch the shop for an hour and I'll go."

Emma's hand froze halfway to her mouth. The toast in her fingers wobbled. She dropped it back onto her plate. "I can't do that."

"Which?" Sophie returned to the stove and cracked another egg into the pan. "Go to the grocery store or watch the shop? If you mean the latter, well, people will have questions, but you can always ask them to stop in again when I'm there. Or you could just go to the grocery store. Surely you've managed to do that on a few occasions." She grinned at Emma.

Emma straightened her spine against the wooden chair back. She couldn't believe Sophie was asking her this. She couldn't believe her sister didn't even think beyond the request. "What if I run into…someone?"

"What, with the shopping cart?" Sophie tucked up to the table with her own breakfast.

"Of course not with the shopping cart," Emma snapped, immediately regretting her temper. "Sorry."

Sophie shrugged off Emma's apology, swallowing the food in her mouth. "I know you didn't mean that, Ems. I know exactly what you meant. And he doesn't live here anymore. He moved away shortly after you did."

Emma's mouth dropped open. Naturally Sophie would have that information. Sophie kept in touch with old friends, whereas Emma…Emma had abandoned them all. Why, however, had Sophie chosen to keep the information to herself?

"You never told me," Emma stated.

Sophie picked up a butter knife and slathered her toast with strawberry jam. "You never asked."

Emma narrowed her eyes. "Did I have to?"

"Yes," said Sophie in a quiet, firm voice, "because, quite frankly, I didn't think you'd want to know right after everything and later I didn't think you'd care."

Emma shoveled her egg into her mouth in silence, mind racing. This was what coming home meant. Rushing memory, old pain, curiosity, unanswered questions, admitting to your little sister you'd failed at your life's work. It wasn't like in the movies, all that sweet nostalgia and hope. It was filled with revelations like this one. Well, at least she'd be able to pick up groceries without worry.

Plowing through her toast, too, Emma chewed noisily and aggressively. At some point Sophie got up and disappeared into the bedroom. When she returned, she was dressed. She had a handwritten list in her hand and several twenty dollar bills. She pushed them toward Emma across the tabletop.

"We can start with this," Sophie said, "and then maybe we can go shopping together later this week. I need to figure out Christmas dinner anyway."

"Right, Christmas dinner," Emma echoed absently. Despite all the decorations in town and the fact Sophie's shop smelled like the holidays incarnate, Christmas seemed as far away as if it had already come and gone. Before Sophie's invite, Emma hadn't even bothered to make plans. She still hadn't bought a single gift for her niece and nephews nor had she ordered the wreath she usually sent to her parents for their front door. She hadn't given any thought whatsoever to the pending celebrations. Except for the cold, the week coming up might as well have been leading to a green midsummer for all the seasonal expectancy she felt.

"Ems, you okay?"

"Absolutely," said Emma, picking up her plate and utensils and heading for the dishwasher. She paused at the sink. There was no window here like you'd see in a house, only a solid wall that someone—probably Sophie—had cleverly disguised with a stenciled depiction of curtains and a window box filled with bright red geraniums.

Emma turned on the water. She ran her plate back and forth beneath the spray, intent on the bouncing droplets.

"Did Jack really marry her, that girl he met in college?" she asked. At her sister's long silence, Emma turned around. The light through the living room windows cast Sophie's face into shadow, but Emma could see her hands, fingers tightly intertwined, knuckles strained and white.

"Yes," Sophie whispered. "Yes, I heard he did."

*　　*　　*

Sophie had more than heard. She'd gone to Jack's wedding.

Closing her eyes, Sophie clutched the candle she called Christmas Snowdrift beneath her nose. She breathed in, seeking calm in the combination of lavender and fir essential oils, vanilla and the lovely, underlying cranberry and citrus hints. Sophie had hoped the subject would never come up. She hadn't known what to say then, she didn't know what to say now.

"That's why we all like your candles, dear," said a voice near the counter. "They smell so wonderful. You look enraptured."

Sophie's lids popped open. Enraptured? Filled with remorse and desperate for forgiveness was more like it—if she could ever let Emma know the truth.

"Thank you, Mrs. Rood. That's very kind," Sophie squeaked.

"I'll take the scent you have there," Mrs. Rood said, pointing at the twenty-ounce jar Sophie held. "Your expression is the best recommendation. Could you gift wrap it for me, please?"

"Happy to." Sophie hurried to the table behind the counter where she kept the gift boxes, wrapping paper and other supplies. With automatic precision she removed the hanging price tag, folded tissue paper around the candle, slipped it into the box and began wrapping, all while visualizing the day she'd bumped into Jack in the post office where he'd been changing his address.

Sophie had always been fond of Jack, always thought him a good guy, kind and honest, despite the breakup with her sister. Sophie's heart had broken almost as much as Emma's to see them split. But saying yes to his hesitant invitation? What had she been thinking? Oddly, keeping the invite to the nuptials and her acceptance hidden from Emma had been the easiest part. Harder had been not telling Emma about Jack's roundabout inquiries regarding Emma's life, how obvious it had been to Sophie that Jack still cared about her sister.

Sophie should have said something to Jack, though, about what she'd recognized. She regretted that most of all. Instead, she'd asked an old high school friend to go to the wedding with her as her 'plus one' and never said a word.

"Sophie, dear, would you mind putting a different bow on the package? The one you're holding clashes horribly."

Sophie glanced down and gulped. "No problem," she murmured and changed the bow out. Afterward, she rang the candle up for Mrs. Rood, slipped the purchase into a bag and wished her a Merry Christmas.

The woman paused on her way out the door. "Love what you did with the window," she said. "The furnishings are charming and the one candle in the center makes a nice statement."

"Thanks," Sophie said. "Not a lot of room in there and I can't really fill the window with candles considering how hard the afternoon sun beats in. Most of them are soy and the jars would end up filled with fragrant wax soup."

Mrs. Rood laughed in understanding. "I'm going to tell a friend of mine about the painted desk and chair set. She has a young daughter I think would absolutely love it."

"Much appreciated," Sophie responded with a wave. "Again, have a wonderful Christmas."

As soon as the woman disappeared along the sidewalk, Sophie dropped her elbows onto the tiled counter and lowered her head into her hands.

She couldn't think about this. What had happened six years ago was inconsequential compared to Emma's current predicament and Sophie's own needs. What did it matter now?

It mattered, she told herself. It did. She'd basically betrayed Emma back then. Something like that didn't go away—it got pushed into a dark and dusty corner waiting for a metaphorical broom to sweep it back out again at the most undesirable time.

Straightening, Sophie brushed her hair from her face. The morning rush had ended and the usual break had arrived before afternoon holiday customers started swarming in. She needed to eat. The baby demanded it.

Sophie crouched and opened the small refrigerator beneath the counter. Rummaging through the contents, she picked a yogurt and yanked it out. She ripped back the lid, swirled the contents with a nearby plastic spoon, and stuck the overfull spoon in her mouth right as the tiny bells over the door jangled.

Bolting to her feet, spoon clamped between her teeth, Sophie mumbled a garbled greeting at the customer silhouetted inside the door.

Only it wasn't just any customer.

It was Jack.

*   *   *

Sixty dollars hadn't gone as far as Emma would have hoped. Emma had two small bags in each hand and a minimal amount of change for Sophie in her jeans pocket. Nevertheless, Emma found herself in remarkably good spirits. Her mood could turn out to be fleeting, but for now she strode down the sidewalk with her head up, breathing in the crisp, cool air like she owned it and admiring the homegrown flare of Connor Falls' holiday décor. Separate from Sophie's list and funds, she'd purchased a roasting chicken and vegetables for side dishes, and planned to make dinner for her sister tonight, at a reasonable hour. It was the least she could do. Sophie had welcomed Emma into her home and into her life without demur. During the next week or two they'd help each other work things out. What were sisters for, if not that?

They might even enjoy a nice, quiet Christmas together.

So far, she hadn't bumped into anyone who'd recognized her. There had been no awkward attempts at playing catch-up. No need to prevaricate or misconstrue. She could have been in Anywhere, USA, rather than the town where she'd grown up under the scrutiny of a community filled with people who had, through the years, witnessed her triumphs and heartbreaks and shame.

Her stomach gave a sudden growl. Emma lifted her arm, bags and all, and tried to shake back her coat sleeve to check the time on her watch. She didn't notice someone had paused on the sidewalk until she plowed right into him.

Exclamations, apologies and extrication ensued.

Emma managed to step away from the man who'd dropped to the sidewalk to snatch at a tin escaped from her grocery bag. Her breath caught at the curve of his ears peeking out from unkempt dark hair. When he stood, her guts rolled down into her toes and back up again to slam hard into her diaphragm.

Leaning toward her, Jack Winters slipped the fallen can back into her bag and straightened.

"Hello, Emma," he said.

His smile revealed not the slightest discomfort at seeing her again. Neither did his eyes, brown and long-lashed and friendly as ever. Had he dismissed everything between them? Maybe he had. Maybe she was the only one plagued by memories like pop-up ads.

"Jack," she said. "How are you?" Her lips had turned to lead, her voice to a breathless sigh. She wanted to kick herself.

"Good," he said. "And you? You look great."

She wanted to say something trivial and light and oh, so unaffected by his presence. What came out was a simple and barely perceptible thank you.

Jack shifted his stance, cocking his hip to one side. Emma recognized the posture. He planned on settling in for conversation. Emma opened her mouth to tell him she had an appointment.

He spoke first. "Sophie said you were in town for the holidays."

"You—you've been talking with Sophie? When?" Emma's cheeks heated in the chill air. How much had Sophie kept from her?

Jack lifted his hand, displaying a striped paper tote with Sophie's store logo on it. "I just bought a candle called Christmas Snowdrift in her store. Sophie said it's the fifth one she's sold today. Popular scent, apparently."

Emma sucked a long breath in through her nose, releasing it slowly. "Present for your wife?"

"My mom, actually," he said, peering into the bag before lowering his hand back to his side. "She's brought up the store so many times I started to figure it was a hint."

"So, first time in there?"

"Yep."

Around his shoulder, Emma spotted her sister standing outside the shop door speaking with an older woman clasping a large bag. Emma narrowed her eyes briefly in Sophie's direction before returning her attention to Jack. "Are you here for Christmas, too? Sophie didn't mention you'd come to spend the holidays with your family."

"I don't think she knew," said Jack, "unless my parents said something to her. She seemed quite surprised to see me, though. Honestly, I haven't seen your sister since—"

"Jack!"

Both Jack and Emma whipped around at Sophie's voice. Sophie hurried toward them, waving something in her hand. When she reached them, she held a postcard-sized object toward Jack. Emma tipped her head to view it and saw it was a

postcard like the one Sophie had sent to her. Sophie turned it over, revealing outlined squares framing the edge, one which had been stamped with a tiny inked candle.

"I meant to give this to you," Sophie stated breathlessly. "I keep forgetting to give them out. You get a stamp for every purchase, and when the card is filled you get a free 5 oz. candle." Her eyes darted in Emma's direction and away again.

"Thanks, Soph," said Jack, tucking the card into his bag. He made a slight, sliding movement to his right, bringing him closer to Emma. She smelled his aftershave, a scent like summertime and warmth, and so very familiar. She bit her lip.

"I have to run," Jack said, taking another step, this one putting him further away. "But I hope...well,

I hope to see you both again while I'm here." He nodded at Sophie and turned toward Emma, planting a quick, light kiss on her forehead before he strode off.

Clutching the groceries, Emma stared after him. He walked in the same manner she remembered, loose, lanky, unhurried. She supposed she expected him to be changed, somehow, rather than so plainly recognizable as the man she'd known. Time had altered him a bit, small transformations in appearance such as the way he wore his hair, the lines around his eyes from squinting into the sun, laughing, living his life. These changes didn't make him different. They made him absolutely Jack in every way.

Not until Sophie had grabbed the two bags from her left hand did Emma realize her eyes had foolishly filled with tears.

Chapter Four

Later that evening, Sophie pulled a box from the guest room closet and handed it to Emma. She'd been keeping an eye on Emma all day, expecting a meltdown. To her surprise, Emma had remained calm, although quiet, and had even helped out in the shop until she'd retreated upstairs to make dinner. Sophie had come up after closing the store to delicious aromas wafting through the kitchen and a carefully set table. Sophie had always been a bit haphazard when it came to the niceties, like napkins. Emma had apparently purchased a pack at the store, rather than resorting to Sophie's use of paper towels. Sophie hadn't let it annoy her. Emma needed the things that made her comfortable right now.

"That one's yours," Sophie said, nodding at the carton in her sister's arms.

Emma dipped her head to study the folded top, brow furrowed. "This is my what?"

"Christmas decorations," Sophie said. "The ones Mom and Dad split up between the four of us kids before they moved."

Emma continued to frown down at the taped-up carton with her name scrawled across the flap in marker. "Okay. I see my name. So what are you doing with them?"

Sophie's lips twisted. "No need to get testy." She pulled out another, larger box, filled not only with the tree ornaments from her parents but the others she'd collected over the years. "You didn't take them, so Judy claimed custody of the box. I asked for it earlier this year."

"Why?"

"So I could make you take them home with you

at some point." Balancing the cumbersome box on her hip, Sophie pushed the closet door shut and headed out to the living room, Emma trailing after.

"Do you even decorate for Christmas?" Sophie asked her as they passed through the kitchen. Dishes were still piled in the sink from dinner, driving Emma crazy, Sophie knew.

"I decorate for Christmas," said Emma testily behind her. "You've seen it."

"I haven't, Ems. Think about it. You've never had any of us for Christmas at your place."

Emma's footsteps stopped. Sophie continued into the living room and lowered her box onto the rug. A six-foot tall evergreen stood to one side before the window, delivered that afternoon from a boy from Luke's Tree Farm. Together, she and Emma had wrestled the tree into the stand before dinner, and wrapped it in twinkling, white bulbs. Right now, fresh balsam competed with the lingering aroma of roast chicken in the air. Sophie was glad the all-day morning sickness had stopped several weeks prior, because even without it she was having trouble dealing with the mix.

"Never?" Emma eventually echoed in frank disbelief.

"Never," Sophie assured her.

On her knees, Sophie tore the tape from the box and folded back the flaps. From the corner of her eye she saw Emma lower herself slowly into a nearby chair, the box with Emma's name on it still in her arms. In spite of the numerous memories to be found in the box nestled in her lap, Emma's gaze remained fixed, wide-eyed, on the floor.

"Ems?"

Emma glanced up. "I'm okay."

"I don't think you are." Sophie didn't believe her sister. In the past, Emma had always been the planner, mapping out her life from the time she was fourteen. Now she'd lost her job, her home, her focus and, as an added bonus, she'd run into Jack Winters today. Okay wasn't on the agenda. In fact, it wasn't allowed. She needed to let it out.

"Really, I'm fine," Emma insisted.

Sophie shook her head and reached into the box by her knees. She pulled out a newspaper-wrapped ornament and held it a moment in her hands. Sophie's attendance at Jack's wedding was bound to come out if Emma ran into him again. Despite the much-needed release of emotion that would likely follow for Emma, Sophie didn't want her to hear it from the man who'd broken her heart. Sophie had considered confession a vague goal for this evening, but visualization had always turned somewhat cartoonish, involving shattered ornaments and a tree toppled onto the floor.

In all honesty, what she wanted most was to avoid adding to Emma's hurt. But Jack had come home for the holidays and expressed a desire to see them both again. The truth couldn't wait much longer.

"I need to tell you about something," said Sophie.

"No," said Emma, "I need to say something first."

At Emma's tone, Sophie flinched a little. Had Jack already mentioned the wedding to Emma? No, how stupid. For one thing, Emma wouldn't have stewed on a revelation like that all day. For another, Emma and Jack couldn't possibly have been talking more than two minutes based on when he'd left the store. They'd probably not gotten past the usual courtesies before Sophie had hustled over to them in a diversionary tactic, waving Jack's postcard.

"Go ahead," Sophie said. "What's up?"

"Did you know Jack was in Connor Falls for Christmas? You said I wouldn't run into him, but maybe you didn't want me to worry—"

Sophie answered without hesitation. "No, I didn't know. Why?"

"I thought…I thought maybe you'd kept in touch

with him."

Time to fess up, Sophie Parsons.

"I haven't, Ems, but—"

"I still love him."

Sophie sighed. She'd suspected as much. "That's a long time to—"

"Love a man who doesn't love me? Tell me about it."

Sophie hadn't planned to say quite those words. What had almost slipped from her mouth had Emma not interrupted was that it was a long time to yearn after what could have been. Despite what Sophie had noted in Jack's behavior the day he asked her to the wedding, he looked happy when he'd come into her store earlier, contented. He'd made the right choice for himself. She and Jack hadn't had a chance to talk about things like his marriage, whether he had kids, all the usual you asked people you haven't seen in a while, but wherever his life had taken him, it seemed the right path.

"Look, Ems, I—"

"I haven't had a bona fide relationship since Jack," Emma continued as if Sophie hadn't spoken.

"I know."

"Then seeing him today…" Emma hung her

head. "I'm hopeless. Absolutely hopeless. What does that say about me as a person that I can't move on? How can I be this way? Argh," she cried out dramatically, trying to force a laugh.

Sophie shuffled across the rug on her knees and took the box from her sister's grasp, setting it on the floor beside the chair. "Aw, Ems, don't be so tough on yourself. Look at me and Ben, if you want an example of not moving on. This ain't no watermelon seed growing in my belly."

With a loud snort, Emma threw a hand up to cover her nose and mouth. Dark hair flying, she threw herself back against the chair cushion in a giggling fit. Sophie followed suit helplessly until she was on the floor clutching her belly.

"It's…not…funny," she gasped.

"So not funny," Emma choked out and went off into another bout of laughter.

At last, breathless and spent and wiping her eyes, Sophie pushed herself up off the floor. "Feel better now?" she asked.

"Better than crying," Emma answered, sucking in air tremulously in an attempt to control the laughter still lurking.

"Good, let's get back to decorating." Sophie reached for the ornament she'd dropped.

"Ben's not married, though."

Pausing with her hand above the wrapped bauble, Sophie frowned. "What's that got to do with anything?"

Emma leaned forward, pressing her fingers into her knees. "You might yet make it work, Soph. Have you thought about that?"

Sophie ripped the newspaper from the ornament, balled it up and tossed it aside. "No, we won't, and yes, I have. Ben and I have discussed it, actually, and I can assure you there's no way. We'll reach some sort of arrangement, because the baby ought to know his or her father. Otherwise, that's it. Nada. Zip."

Sobering, Emma pulled the tape from her box and began rummaging through it. "But he sure is beautiful, isn't he?"

"I assume you don't mean Ben."

"Well, he's not bad either. No, I mean Jack, naturally."

"He'll do," said Sophie. Emma had always raved about how beautiful Jack was. A handsome man, he also possessed certain qualities, like Emma, that made him special, qualities that went beyond physical attributes. This was what Emma meant when she called Jack Winters beautiful. Sophie wondered if

Emma would ever see him any other way.

"What's that you got there?" Sophie asked, nodding at a smaller carton Emma had removed from the main one.

Emma rolled back the crinkled newsprint. With an astonished exclamation, she pulled out an ornament made to resemble a snow globe, the wooden base coated in gold-flecked paint and the globe fashioned from clear, thin, crystal glass. An exquisite porcelain nativity graced the interior.

"I remember this," Emma whispered. "Weren't there four, each with something different inside?"

Sophie smiled at Emma's reaction. "Yep," she said. "They came from Germany. We all ended up with one. Aren't you glad we've kept your box safe all this time?"

Emma leaned down and hugged Sophie hard, holding the ornament at a cautious distance above their colliding bodies. "I love you, Soph."

"I love you, too," Sophie answered. "You know that."

Sophie felt her sister stiffen momentarily in her arms. Emma pulled back to look Sophie in the eye.

"You know I love you," Sophie said again, dropping her arms.

Emma's lids lowered. When she lifted them

again, wariness had replaced her misty-eyed sentimentality. "What is it? What did you want to talk to me about?"

Sophie hesitated, picking at the metal hook on the ornament she still held in her hand. She didn't really want to ruin their special evening, but she should have told Emma long ago. If she held back now it would only be worse, what with Emma's disclosure about Jack. Sophie couldn't put off telling Emma another minute.

"You know when I said I'd heard Jack got married? I didn't just hear. I was there."

*   *   *

With extraordinary care, Emma lowered the snow globe ornament to the side table and released her hold on it. The glass was delicate and her grip at that moment perilous.

"I ran into him at the post office a few weeks before the date," Sophie explained, rushing, it seemed, to get the words out. "He invited me out of politeness and I said yes."

Emma gave this full thought for about five seconds. She didn't require more time to understand her sister's rationalization held an obvious flaw. "You could have said no. He would have understood. As you said, he was only being polite."

Sophie rocked back a little over her heels. After a moment, she got to her feet and hung the glass bauble she'd been holding on the tree. Folding her arms across her chest, she took a single step back to study it, as if the thing's position deserved all her attention. Emma waited, but what she really wanted was to throw something at her sister. She eyed Sophie's discarded newspaper and decided it wouldn't have the desired effect.

"I know I could have," Sophie said without looking at her. "I know I could have said no. Out of loyalty to you, I should have. But I've always liked Jack and no matter how hard I tried to muster dislike on your behalf, I've never been able to do it. You were over and done with at that point and it wasn't like he'd been some horrible monster. It killed me the two of you had broken up. I always thought he'd make the perfect brother-in-law and I was quite aware how much you loved him. But honestly, you'd drifted apart when you went away to school. I don't think he ever fully realized how much he hurt you. And I don't think he ever stopped caring, either."

Well, ouch.

Emma shifted in her seat. "But you didn't think to tell me," she said.

Sophie bent and pulled out another ornament, studying it in her hands. "I thought about it quite often, to be honest. I decided it was best if I didn't say anything. I figured Jack wasn't going to enter either of our lives again and in the end it wouldn't matter. Naturally, he would walk into my shop today and meet you on the sidewalk right after."

Sophie hung the blown glass Santa to the right and below the first ornament. "Almost like fate," she added in a mutter, reaching for the next.

"Pretty cruel stroke of fate, then, considering how I'm feeling," Emma said.

"Fate's not always kind."

Emma pushed up from the chair and began emptying her box, setting ornaments on the cushion side by side.

"How are you feeling?" Sophie asked, having hung a dozen more decorations while Emma unpacked.

"Feeling?"

"Exactly. How are you feeling right now?"

Emma moved to stand beside her sister, contemplating Sophie's arrangement on the tree. It had looked haphazard from where Emma had been sitting, but she recognized a deliberate pattern now. Rather than spoil what had been begun, she handed Sophie the frosted glass pear dangling from her finger.

Emma gave the question thought, handing Sophie ornament after ornament from both boxes. Each decoration hung brought back memories. Christmas as a child had been filled with enchantment, recollection making each one perfect rather than what they probably really had been—hectic, emotional, exhausting and fraught with childish bickering. Yet the more she remembered, the more Emma understood what brought families back together. Moments like this, for example, as she worked side by side with her sister to create a new memory. And as with youthful Christmases, Emma might remember only that and forget the pain of this day as the years went by.

Emma took another ornament from the box. She peeled off the newsprint. Her mouth widened into a smile. Crouching, she hung the angel she'd made in school near the bottom. She couldn't believe her parents had held onto it or that they'd packed it up for her. Giving the paper mache creation a knock with her pointer finger, she watched the glitter sparkle in the light before she straightened to stand beside Sophie again.

"When I first bumped into Jack today I was shocked and a bit angry," Emma said, "but it was really good to see him."

Sophie reached into the small space between them and squeezed Emma's hand. "Wouldn't it be nice if everybody stayed? If no one ever went away?"

*   *   *

Yes, thought Sophie, tracking car lights across the bedroom ceiling. Wouldn't it be nice if everybody stayed? Life didn't work that way. Families grew, evolved, individual members moved into their own spheres.

She remembered the day she'd decided she wouldn't come back. She'd met Ben by then, had been flying full steam ahead with school, her future, her love. Mom and Dad were already talking about moving to North Carolina. Sophie's siblings were waffling about whether one of them should buy their parents' home, keep the roots going. It had been Sophie who'd encouraged them all to take flight.

Why had she done that?

Connor Falls didn't always fit into the inevitability the world had fashioned. Many folks stuck around. Generations stayed within its boundaries. The fledgling young often returned. She had. She'd returned with a purpose, to regain the sense of home she'd lost.

Christmas was supposed to be a time when families gathered, friends stopped by and all were welcome. Five Christmases had come and gone without every Parsons member, by blood or marriage, roosting somewhere together. Someone was always missing. Most recently, it had been Sophie and Emma.

Lying in the dark, waiting for the next roaming headlight to shine through the wooden shutters, Sophie pondered the path her life had taken. Many acquaintances viewed her as quite insane, leaving a good job for the dicey territory of the self-employed. Sophie had no regrets on that level. She was happy, happier than she'd been in a very long time. Her ability to look after a child was assured within the shop's confines, as well. Many neighboring stores were in similar circumstance, family-run, children underfoot. She would make it work.

No, it was Emma who worried her.

Self-assured Emma, elegant Emma… Heartbroken Emma.

Sophie might not be able to do anything about the emotional issues related to Jack or whatever had happened at work, but she sure as heck had a market for Emma's talents, if she could only convince her to stick around.

Turning over in bed, shutting her eyes against car lights, Sophie heard a noise beyond the creaking of her bed frame. She sat up, shoved her legs over the mattress edge, feet searching for slippers before she even discerned the nature.

"Ems?" she called, but not loudly. The noise hadn't come from the apartment. It had come from downstairs.

Oh hell.

Sophie slapped around on the nightstand, feeling for her cell phone. She dropped to her knees and rummaged beneath the bed. Nothing. Where had she left it?

The only landline she possessed was in the store, and that wouldn't do her any good now.

Kitchen. Her cell phone had to be in the kitchen. She scurried toward the nightlight's soft glow beside the sink, listening hard for another sound from below. Hearing a bump, she swore softly. Why would someone break into her store? No one could possibly believe they'd be seizing a fortune from her register and candles weren't exactly a hot ticket item on whatever market burglars traded their wares.

Unable to locate her phone, she pivoted abruptly, heading for the guest room. Emma always kept her cell phone glued to her side. No need to waste time.

Without knocking, Sophie threw open the door. Emma's bed was empty.

Chapter Five

Sophie's shop was *magic*. Emma couldn't explain it. Quiet as she could she'd crept around peering at the merchandise, lifting candle lids to smell the fragrances, examining labeled lotion ingredients by the streetlight, admiring the packaging in which the soaps were wrapped, studying the enchanting scenes on furnishings. She'd peeked in at a roomy, well-organized workspace where all these things were created and prepared. Finally, she'd taken a decorated child's chair and, after ascertaining she'd do no damage, set it a few feet beyond where the light through the window cast myriad shadows. For the past half hour she'd been sitting on it in the darkness.

Sophie had done this all herself. Emma couldn't imagine the drive, the determination, the ability to take a dream and make it reality like this. It had to be tough, being both creative and business-minded. For Emma, the undertaking would be darned near impossible.

A couple passed outside, making their way from some late night assignation. Their voices vibrated against the glass like music and drifted away into the snowfall—a mere flurry—dancing through the glow from the curbside streetlamp. A few moments later church bells rang softly in the air. Emma listened as they finished their gentle melody and chimed the hour.

"Midnight."

Emma jumped. Head snapping around, she spotted her sister in the opening to the workroom, where the stairs to the apartment were located.

"Lucky I checked your room first," Sophie said, "or I would have been coming down here with a baseball bat."

Emma snorted, lips curving. "No you wouldn't have. You'd have been on the phone to the police. At least, that better be your first course of action. I don't ever want to learn you've charged down into this shop when you thought an intruder was inside."

"I hear you, sis," Sophie said, coming closer. She shuffled to a stop beside Emma with her feet clad in fuzzy red-nosed reindeer slippers.

"Or," said Emma, "just let the burglar spot you in those. You'd be picking him up off the floor."

"Ha. Ha." Sophie lowered herself next to Emma's borrowed chair. She stretched her legs out, waggling her feet from side to side. "I think they're cute. What are you doing down here?"

"Sitting."

"I see that," said Sophie. "Why?"

"Thinking."

A loud and undisguised sigh escaped Sophie's lips. She drew up one knee and plopped her chin on it, wrapping her arms around her bent leg. "About what?"

"Everything."

Sophie didn't bother to respond. Several more people passed the window, one singing a lively Christmas carol while another told him to shut up. In a moment their boisterous conversation had vanished into the night's singular quiet. Emma could hear her sister's steady, soft breathing.

"It's a whole world out there," Emma said.

"Well…yeah," said Sophie.

"And it's almost like a sanctuary in here."

Sophie rolled her head on her knee, turning to look at her. Reflected light gleamed in Sophie's eyes. "That's an odd thing to say."

Emma looked at her sister and away. "Not really. You've created this haven for yourself, Soph. Not to hide away, but to work and live and thrive in the way you want. You've taken a dream and made it reality. You should be proud of what you've done. I am."

Wriggling her bottom across the floor, Sophie pressed close to Emma's legs. She encircled Emma's bare ankle with her fingers and squeezed. "Thank you."

"Not a problem," said Emma. "Just calling it like I see it."

"And what about you?"

"Me?"

"Yup."

An anticipatory thrum, almost fear, vibrated through Emma's temporary peace. Emma's problems couldn't be easily catalogued, repaired, solved. Her life had tumbled into a disastrous mess. She hadn't left her job on good terms, would probably never get a reference worth a damn. All her recent designs were company property and both anger and sorrow had muddied her creative vision into non-existence. Add Jack Winters' current arrival into that mix and you had one, huge cocktail of hopelessness.

Sitting up, Sophie cupped a hand around her ear and leaned sideways. "What was that, Ems?"

Emma eyed her sister askance. "You're not five anymore. Spit it out."

"You need a place, too. A place to breathe for a bit, to get your life in order. You'd like to stick around."

"Oh, is that what you think I'm saying?"

"No," answered Sophie, "that's what I say you're thinking."

Emma stood. She grabbed the chair and returned it to its place. "Lovely piece," she said, to change the subject. "Nice and sturdy. Judy would like that for Alice. You should talk her into buying it."

Biting her lip, Emma watched the light snowfall through the window. Sophie thought she could read people so well. She always had. What made her assume she knew what Emma was thinking, about anything? Sure, Emma needed to come up with a plan to bring her life back under control, but here, in Connor Falls? No. After the holidays, she'd be on her way…to where, she had no idea, but she was determined to have a strategy in place by New Year's.

Her gaze slid once more around the shop. Could she do something like this? Was she capable? Not here, of course. Not in Connor Falls. But somewhere…

Sophie suddenly scrambled upright, beckoning her across the store with a waving hand. "I want to show you something."

Reluctantly, Emma followed Sophie to a cabinet Emma hadn't noticed in her perusal. "When'd this get here? Did you have it delivered today?"

The small curio cabinet stood about four feet tall and had clearly been made many years ago, sometime, perhaps, in the early twentieth century. The wood was dark, the short legs narrow and fluted, the glass on both sides curved. An ornate metal knob on the glass at the front showed where the door opened. The shelves inside were empty.

"I bought it when I moved here, at a flea market." Sophie ran her hand over the top. "It's been in the workroom. I've always had big plans for it."

"Plans? Like painting it?"

"No, not painting it. Unless you think I should?"

"Me?" Emma studied the curio again, confused. "Why would it be up to me?"

Reaching past her, Sophie grabbed the little knob between her thumb and middle finger and tugged the door open. She reached inside. Emma had been wrong. The cabinet wasn't empty. Sophie pulled a folded cardstock sign from the center shelf and held it out to her.

"What's this?" Emma asked.

"Look at it," said Sophie.

Emma brought the card over to the window, turning the cream-colored paper toward the light. Blurred snowflake shadows swirled across four words inscribed by hand using a thick calligraphy pen.

Jewelry by Emma Parsons.

*　　*　　*

Perhaps the middle of the night hadn't been the best time to bring her idea up to Emma. To be honest, she hadn't been able to tell from Emma's reaction whether any other time would have been better. Their conversation beforehand had made it seem like the right moment, though. However, Sophie's perception had probably been skewed due to a lack of sleep two nights running.

Emma, on the other hand, had decided to sleep in this morning, right through breakfast. She was up now, though. Sophie could hear her moving about in the apartment. Footsteps, a chair sliding, water running through the pipes into the shower. Across the shop the curio cabinet Sophie had moved out from the workshop the day before looked stark and forlorn rather than the way she'd imagined it many times since purchase.

Believing Emma would be content working from Sophie's store had been foolish. Foolish and impractical. Emma couldn't make a living from whatever she'd sold through the Chandlery, especially considering what she'd been earning. But they would have been doing something together.

Sophie frowned at the cabinet, recognizing her own selfishness in her wishes. She would sand and paint the stupid thing. An antiqued, crackled finish in ivory with a lavender floral motif could work. But she'd been envisioning the cabinet filled with Emma's perfect designs all these months. Something made just for the store. It was tough to consider the piece used for anything else.

A clunk on the counter recalled Sophie to the

customers moving about her shop.

"These gift baskets are a splendid idea. I'll take both, one for each of my daughters-in-law. Don't need them wrapped, but could you put on a nice bow?"

Sophie chose two from the box and rang up the customer. She remembered to stamp the free candle card and put everything in a bag. Wishing the woman a merry Christmas, Sophie spotted Emma making her way from the back room with a knit hat shoved down on her damp hair. She slowed by the curio cabinet, bent and peered inside, and moved on, straight for the door.

"Emma—" Sophie began. Her sister left without looking back.

"Sophie, was that your sister?"

"Oh, Mrs. Nolan, hi," Sophie said, belatedly recognizing the woman who had come to wait at the register. "Yes, that was Emma. She…she had to run out somewhere."

"I haven't seen her in years. Does she still make that exquisite jewelry? If she's got anything for sale, I'd love to take a look. You'll let her know I asked after her, won't you? And yes, I want both of those, and this one, too," Jeanette Nolan said as Sophie lifted two candles questioningly. Sophie rang them all up, wrapped them in tissue paper for safety, and slipped them in a bag.

Once Mrs. Nolan walked away, Sophie's focus moved again to the empty curio cabinet.

She'd told Emma last night there would be a market in this town for her jewelry. She'd told her, too, there were other outlets, including the website she was paying Todd from the bookstore to help her build. Emma hadn't wanted to hear it. She said her interest in that industry was finished. The harder Sophie tried to convince Emma what she did wasn't industry, but art, the more Emma displayed no inclination to listen.

"Like a two-year-old," Sophie muttered, reaching to take another bite from the apple she'd brought down with her when she'd opened the store.

"Excuse me?"

"Sorry," Sophie apologized to the man who popped up from behind a display. He stood about her height and looked vaguely familiar. "Talking to myself."

"No worries," he said. "I'm sorry as well. I was blatantly eavesdropping on your conversation with the woman who just left. I heard you say your sister makes jewelry."

Sophie straightened, putting the apple back down onto its soggy napkin. "She di—does. Outstanding jewelry. She worked for a company based in Atlanta but has decided to take a break from the manufacturing angle to focus again on the artistic side of her craft."

Heck, if she was going for public relations on her sister's behalf, she might as well make it good. It would have been better if Emma had been here to speak for herself, but Sophie held a suspicion she would have blown this guy off rather than discuss what she'd been doing.

The man approached the counter. Beneath a thatch of sandy hair, he possessed a pleasant face, friendly and open. He had an affable manner, too, with a comfortable, calming smile as he extended his hand to her. "The name's Will. Will English." He shook her hand and released it so he could reach into his pocket. He placed a business card on the counter a few inches from her apple. "Don't let me stop you. I can talk while you eat."

"Will English, Sophie Parsons at your service," Sophie said, making new grooves in the fruit with her front teeth. "And I'm starving," she added around a mouthful, "so thank you."

"Nice shop. I assume you're the Sophie in Sophie's Chandlery?"

She nodded her assent, still chewing.

"New?"

"Second holiday season," Sophie said, covering her mouth while she spoke. "Opened a year ago September."

Will seemed undeterred by the fact she was answering him in bits around masticated apple. He smiled. "You're doing well."

"Trying," she said, lowering her fruit.

"Eat," said Will. "I'll just look around a bit more."

Sophie kept an eye on him as she quickly finished off the apple. He bent to peer at a small, painted jewelry box and straightened with his profile in view for the first time. Tossing core and napkin into the trash, Sophie hastened around the counter. "Are you any relation to the woman who runs the bookstore?"

He turned with a start. "I'm her cousin. I didn't think there was that much family resemblance."

"Your profile," said Sophie. "Allie and I went to school together."

"I'll mention I stopped in your store when she and I have dinner tonight."

"Great. Tell her I said hi." Sophie stood a moment in awkward indecision, wondering how to bring up Emma and her jewelry again.

"Do you have any photos of your sister's work?" Will asked, as if reading her mind.

"As a matter of fact," said Sophie, "I do. Hold on."

Sophie returned to the counter and grabbed her cell phone. She flipped through the photos to find the most recent. Emma hadn't exactly shared them with her. Sophie had happened upon an article about Emma's company in a magazine at the dentist's office and excitedly taken pictures with her phone. She held up the cell and showed them to Will, one at a time.

"You're very proud of your sister, aren't you?" Will said, taking the phone from her to study one in particular more closely.

"I am," Sophie stated, lifting her chin.

He handed the cell back. "With good reason. These are fabulous. Each piece seems to possess a stark but lovely contrast of fragility and strength."

"Just like Emma," Sophie said, before she had a chance to edit the words escaping her mouth. She sucked in a breath and made a face.

"Don't worry," Will said with a chuckle. "I won't tell. Have her call me, will you?"

"Sure," said Sophie. "I'll do my best."

He cocked an eyebrow at her, confused by her words.

"What I mean is that she's a little busy with the holidays, but I'll give her your card and hound her."

"Thanks." He started to turn away but spun back with a sheepish grin. "I almost forgot my reason for coming here. I need a gift for my sister. She's in love with your beeswax lotion. I think the scent is called something and ivy?"

"Right over here," Sophie said, stepping out from behind the counter. By the time he left, Will had purchased not only the lotion but matching soap and a square votive candle. Sophie boxed and wrapped them for him. In the meantime, several more patrons entered the store, all waiting with questions. Forty-five minutes passed before Sophie realized she hadn't yet looked at Will's business card, nor had Emma returned.

Sophie held the card under the desk lamp beside the register. Her breath stilled in her lungs. She picked up her phone to call Emma, set it on the counter again. Not a phone call kind of conversation. This could change everything.

*　*　*

Emma had had to drive quite a distance away to find what she needed. The small town where she'd grown up had somehow avoided the sprawl of new construction all around, while still remaining viable.

Upon leaving the town limits, one found smaller neighborhoods, or two- to nearly three-hundred-year-old homes nestled in the valley bordered by hills and open fields, or large working farms with woodlands in between. In order to reach anything resembling the shopping she'd gotten used to in her adult life, Emma took to the main road and followed it for twenty-five minutes. Now, laden with several bags and a slightly guilty conscience due to the money she'd spent, Emma headed back to Connor Falls.

The investment could be worth it in the end, if only for the happiness she might bring her sister. Even though she'd rejected Sophie's suggestion, a sleepless night to reconsider had revealed its merit. Emma hadn't planned on returning to what Sophie termed her "art"— at least not yet—and if Sophie was hoping for holiday sales it was a little late, but Emma had never seen her sister so earnest, so centered, so in control. Anything she could do to help with that made sense.

Emma took her time returning, enjoying the landscape. Even mostly leafless, the hills had a lovely, rounded appearance. In the summer, they would be green and lush. She'd worked one early autumn after school in an apple orchard. She'd nearly forgotten. Hard work, it had been, but there had been something special about being outside enjoying the seasonal change as she and a few other kids labored among the regulars in the orchard. If she recalled correctly, her biceps had become rather impressive that year as well.

Spotting the sign for Luke's Tree Farm, Emma impulsively took the right. Turning at the entrance to the huge evergreen farm, Emma maneuvered with care past people lined up at the wrapping machine waiting for their trees to be secured for transport. Many put off tree-buying until the last minute. To ensure their trees remained fresh through the holidays, Emma supposed, or was it their particular tradition? The Parsons had always gotten their tree early, the longer to enjoy it even if the evergreen was shedding its needles all over the floor by January. Emma, however, hadn't had a Christmas tree in her apartment, ever. It had seemed like too much trouble in a space already cramped. She'd been surprised when Sophie had one brought into her small place, and yet when they'd finished decorating the tree it had been more than beautiful. It had made Emma feel like she'd come home.

Home. Connor Falls was not her home. Not anymore.

Emma snorted through her nose, pulling into a parking spot on the graveled lot. What a ridiculous sentiment from the woman who was essentially homeless.

Wreaths decorated and undecorated lined the exterior barn wall. Emma climbed from the car and went over to examine them. She tugged on the needles, checking for freshness as she studied the pine cones, dried flowers and holly branches adorning a select group. Other greens had been added, giving the wreaths additional texture and interest. As she mentally calculated whether there would be enough time to package one and ship it to her parents, she felt a light pressure on her arm.

"Emma?"

Emma gasped and spun around. "Jack!"

"I'm sorry," he said. "Did I scare you?"

"No, no, just startled me," Emma stammered. "What are you doing here?" What a dim-witted question, almost accusatory. "Are you shopping for a tree?" she added, hoping to sound more reasonable.

Jack reached past her with a smile to flip over the price tag on the wreath next to the one she'd been studying. He looked windblown and fit and she wanted to smack herself for noticing. "Nope," he said, "just a wreath for my old neighbor. I noticed his door is still barren and he doesn't get around much these days. I thought I'd surprise him with it this afternoon."

Jack Winters, always unfailingly thoughtful. Even when they'd broken up there had been no unkind words, no finger pointing, only quietly stated fact. Emma remembered trying to provoke him. Why? Perhaps because then she could have justified it all.

"That's very nice of you," Emma said. She glanced past him to the lot, where several children were running between the people chatting as they waited to get their trees bound. Jack had wanted children. They'd talked about it on and off. She wondered if his wife and any offspring might be among the tree shoppers. Somehow, she couldn't bring herself to ask.

"I'm late with gifts this year," she said instead. "I'm hoping I can get this wreath to my parents in time."

He shrugged, tilting his head with a small shake.

"What?" she said. "You don't think I can?"

"You're probably better off ordering one from a florist, to be on the safe side."

He was right, of course. She usually did just that. What on earth had made her stop to buy a fresh one from Luke's?

Because, a little voice inside her head whispered annoyingly, a purchase from Connor Falls would have been special—for her parents and for her. Connor Falls had been their home as a family.

Emma let out a breath in a sigh.

"You okay, Emma?"

"Yeah…"

"I don't think you are." Jack lifted his wreath off the nail and held it at his side. The wintery scent filled Emma's nostrils, prompting a strange, sad longing. "Want to get a cup of coffee?" he said. "I'm happy to be whatever ear you need."

Her head jerked up, eyes meeting his. Compassion and concern marked his expression. She wanted so very badly to say yes, to sit across from him at some small table sipping hot coffee, communing in a bubble like they used to, telling him about her life. But her life wasn't part of his anymore, and his wasn't hers. She couldn't pretend any differently. She had to stop looking back.

"Another time," she said, sidling toward her car.

"Emma."

She lifted a hand, waved and moved a little more quickly. She didn't want to be rude. She only wanted to get away from there before he said something that might make her stay.

"Emma, please."

Emma stopped. She looked at him, at a

countenance no longer displaying concern so much as regret. "Jack, I—"

"I'm not married anymore, Emma. You don't need to run away."

Everything in Emma went still, as if time had stopped. She didn't need to ask him to repeat what he'd said. She'd heard him quite plainly. His words had rushed into her skin, her molecules, like quick-drying cement. She stood rooted to the spot. She couldn't even breathe.

Had this been some romantic movie, they would have rushed into each other's arms while sappy music rose to a heartbreaking crescendo. But this was no movie. This was real life. He stood with his wreath in his hand, looking unsure why he'd spoken. She worked to wriggle free from shock and managed a step back. Her mouth moved. Speech came out.

"That doesn't make a difference, Jack," she said. "It can't."

Turning her back on him, Emma hurried across the lot and into her car. Numbly, she backed out, eyes on Jack in her rear view mirror. He hadn't moved from the spot where she'd left him, but he was watching her. She looked away, pulling out onto the road.

I'm not married anymore, Emma.

The phrase circled inside her head, a wispy, clicking insect in a glass jar. She wanted to release it, let it go, but instead it remained trapped and battering against its boundaries. She needed to study it, she supposed. To figure out what the change meant.

But it meant nothing. Like she'd said, his marital status couldn't make a difference. Not after all this time. Not after all she'd put herself through. The latter was her fault, of course. No one had made her feel the way she did. No one had forced her into the mental and emotional gyrations. Certainly Jack hadn't.

Not that she'd spent all the intervening years longing for the man she'd lost. That would have been scary, in retrospect. But whenever she'd thought about Jack it had been with fondness, regret and a kind of bereavement she'd never quite shaken.

"Focus on the road, loser," Emma chastised herself when she nearly ran a stop sign. The distance from Luke's Tree Farm to Connor Falls couldn't have been more than two miles and yet it had turned into the longest two miles of Emma's life—or at least the one requiring the most concentration.

I'm not married anymore, Emma. You don't need to run away.

Those two sentences from Jack's mouth had been

quite revealing, truth be told. He seemed to have recognized the emotional baggage she'd been carrying around. Or was it uttered in reaction to the moment, when he realized she couldn't even manage something as simple as having coffee with him?

Banging on the steering wheel with her open palm, Emma made her way through town to the narrow street where Sophie had her store. She pulled the car into a parking space and, with the engine still running, sat behind the wheel gazing blankly through the windshield at her past.

There'd been a time, perhaps prematurely considering their ages, when she and Jack had talked in a rather permanent way about their future. They'd even found a house—not for sale—they both would joke about as if it would someday be their own, teasing each other about white picket fences and gardens and sandboxes. Right here in Connor Falls. Emma supposed she should thank Jack for that, being the deciding factor in her exodus. If not for him, she probably would never have left at all. Of all her siblings, she alone had been the one who might have stayed. The irony wasn't lost on her.

Chapter Six

Around midday, Sophie started to wonder if her sister was coming back. She hadn't left with any of her things, though, Sophie reminded herself. And she wouldn't do that. She wouldn't just walk out without a word. Besides, where would she go?

When the store quieted down, Sophie put the be-right-back sign on the door and ran upstairs to use the bathroom and to make a quick cheese sandwich. She made two, in case her sister showed in time to eat one. If not, well, she certainly wouldn't complain about eating the second sandwich, as well.

When she returned to the shop balancing two plates, she discovered Emma's face peering into the interior from beneath a curved hand pressed against the door glass. Emma lifted a fist to knock as Sophie rushed over to unlock the door. Snatching up several shopping bags and a cardboard box, Emma struggled inside and hurried past her. Without speaking, she deposited everything on the counter.

Sophie followed her over, holding a plate out. "Hungry?"

Emma glanced at her and away with a subdued head shake. Her eyes were red-rimmed, her nose pink.

"Ems, you've been crying."

"I don't want to talk about it."

"Fine," said Sophie, placing the plate on the counter among the bags. "Eat a sandwich then."

After several seconds, Emma poked a finger at the bread, lifting the top slice. "What is it?"

"American cheese and mustard. Nothing fancy, but it won't kill you."

Emma snorted, took a bite and set the sandwich back on the plate. "Thank you," she mumbled.

"No problem," Sophie responded, starting in on her own. She indicated the bags with a chin jerk. "What's all this?"

"Stuff."

Sophie rolled her eyes at her sister's back. "What kind of stuff?"

Emma didn't answer. One by one she pulled out the bags' contents and placed everything on the counter. Eventually Sophie understood as she recognized with some surprise the artist's hand mannequins and facial models, together with more typical jewelry displays being arrayed across the tile countertop. Emma opened the cardboard box and removed various pieces of jewelry. Sophie remembered Emma had decided not to bother bringing that particular box in from the trunk.

As if reading her thoughts, Emma spoke. "The company didn't want these designs. They're mine to do with as I please."

"More fool they, for turning those down. They're beautiful."

Emma thanked her, voice quiet.

"So you've decided to set up something in your cabinet?" Sophie tried to keep her tone light. Emma seemed quite fragile at the moment. She looked as though she might burst into tears at the slightest provocation. "I'm really glad."

"Me, too," said Emma, still avoiding her eye. "But I won't…it's only…even after I leave I can send you pieces, if you want."

"Of course, I want. That would be great." She didn't say anything else, finishing her sandwich in silence while Emma arranged the jewelry for display. At one point, her sister's hands shook. What on earth had happened while she'd been out?

"Ems."

"Help me carry these, will you?" Emma picked up a hand mannequin upon which three bracelets had been draped over the palm and one slouched around the wrist. "Do you have hang tags? I'll price them all. I'll need your guidance on that."

Sophie grabbed what she could and preceded Emma to the cabinet, where she piled everything from her arms on top before opening the door. "I'll get you the tags and a pen. You set it up how you think best. I have some lights for inside. Just run the cords through the holes in the back."

Emma squatted on the floor, studying the interior. She stuck her head inside, possibly looking for the holes Sophie had mentioned. "How can you be so nice to me after my asinine response to your offer last night?" Emma asked, voice muffled by her position.

"I'm not nice," Sophie responded. "I just know a good thing when I see it."

Emma said nothing. Her shoulders drooped. After a moment they began to tremble. Yanking her head from the cabinet, Emma slumped over her knees, her face in her hands. With an exclamation Sophie dropped to the floor beside her. She pushed the hair back from her sister's face.

"Ems, what is it? What's happened?"

"I—" Emma sniffed and gulped, struggling for control. "I'm sorry," she said, looking up, her eyes and cheeks awash with tears. She wiped the moisture away with spread fingers. "I hope no customers come in. This would make one pretty picture."

"Talk to me, Ems. Please," Sophie begged. It killed her seeing Emma like this. Emma had always been strong—or had Sophie been mistaken? Sometimes overwhelmed people put on the bravest face. From what Emma had mentioned regarding recent events, she was dealing with a lot. Something today appeared to have pushed her to the breaking point.

"It's nothing," Emma said, shaking her head. She started placing items in the display cabinet without much notice as to order.

"You can stay with me as long as you like," said Sophie. "For as long as you need. I'm not chasing you out. I—I like having you around."

"That would wear thin before long, I'm sure."

Emma reached up for another piece. Sophie yanked the necklace and display form from her reach and held them against her chest. "Why would you say that?"

Dropping her empty hands onto her thighs, Emma frowned. "I'm not good company right now. There's a lot I need to sort out. I should have been doing that for a long while, but I got caught up in life, you know?"

She met Sophie's gaze, brown eyes dark and wounded. An ache settled into Sophie's heart. "You'll find your way again, sis," she whispered.

"I don't have a job. I don't have a home. My friends, well, let's just say they're not very happy with me at the moment. I've taken such huge steps away from my family I'm not sure I can close the gap. And today, today I felt as if I got dumped down a rabbit hole. I'm still sitting in the dark at the bottom wanting very much to climb back out to daylight, but I'm not sure how."

Sophie's mouth opened. Breath came out but

nothing else. Emma returned to arranging the cabinet. Sophie watched her, recognized the determination to slough off her troubles. That wasn't going to work. Not this time. "Am I...am I allowed to argue with you?" Sophie asked.

Emma grunted. "Feel free," she said. Her lips twisted.

"You have a home, if you want it," said Sophie. "I don't know why your friends aren't happy with you, but they'll get over it, if they're really friends. Your family will always be your family. There's not much you can do about that. As far as a job, hold on a second, I'll be right back."

Sophie hurried to the counter, grabbed the jewelry remaining on the tiles together with the business card from Will English. She dropped the bangles and bracelets and exquisite necklaces beside the rest on the cabinet top and shoved the business card at Emma.

Emma took the card slowly, as if it might burn. "What is this?"

Sophie sighed in exasperation. "Look at the card, Ems, will you? Will English is the buyer for Hannah's and I'm pretty sure he wants your jewelry."

*   *   *

Hannah's was Connor Falls' one and only department store. The store had been around for more than eighty years. Emma knew it probably never would have survived on its own in this small town, except that long ago Hannah's had been the place where all the neighboring communities came to shop as well. People in this area possessed loyalty to reputation and quality and both had assured longevity for Hannah's even through times when it could be said not to matter.

Emma turned the card over several times in her fingers, as if something might appear on the back side to explain why this guy had left it with Sophie, how he knew about Emma's work. Well, perhaps that was obvious. Sophie had told him. But how had the subject come up?

Above her, Sophie continued to stare. Emma could feel it as surely as if Sophie stood there tapping on her head. She supposed Sophie expected this turn of events to change everything, but it hadn't. It couldn't. Everything had gotten so complicated, like a knot in a thread. One thing wouldn't unravel it. In fact, one more thing might break it.

The bell rang over the door. Sophie had no choice but to attend to the customer. As soon as her sister walked away, Emma released a held breath. With deliberation, she continued to arrange jewelry in the open cabinet. The exchange between Sophie and the customer drifted into hearing, but she didn't let the content into her thoughts. She'd lost it twice now in the past half hour in sniveling weakness. She needed to hold herself together, finish what she'd set out to do when she left Sophie's apartment this morning. It had made sense to her then. Nothing much made sense to her now.

Jack wasn't married anymore. Divorced, she'd assumed, but she hadn't—she wouldn't—ask.

Suddenly she stopped dead, clutching a necklace in her hand. What if it had been something more terrible, a more enduring loss? She hadn't even stuck around long enough to find out. What was *wrong* with her?

She closed her eyes, remembering Jack's face in the rearview at Luke's. She'd professed to still love him and yet had not taken five minutes to discover the pain he might be in. He'd offered to listen to her over coffee. She'd walked away without a similar courtesy. They didn't have to be friends. They didn't have to be anything. But they had been once. That should count for something, because, thanks to Jack's generous nature, they'd never been enemies.

A bracelet had gotten tangled with another. Emma gently extricated the two pieces, taking a moment to listen now to the conversation between Sophie and her customer. Every time Emma witnessed an interaction between Sophie and a patron, she recognized her sister's easy rapport with everyone who walked through the door, friendly and kind and welcoming. She seemed happy, truly happy, and at home in her environment. Emma envied her the comfort she'd found.

She couldn't decide, however, if this was something Sophie had always possessed, perpetually carried it around inside. Perhaps it had been enhanced by her return to Connor Falls. Emma figured her sister would like her to believe the latter. She seemed determined to make Emma feel some reconnection to the place where they'd all grown up. Even this cabinet filled with Emma's jewelry appeared designed to that purpose.

Pulling the business card from the shelf where she'd laid it down, Emma studied it with her teeth in her lip. Had Sophie somehow arranged this? That would explain a lot. Like how this guy had even heard of Emma. Emma didn't like being manipulated. Who did?

Glancing over her shoulder at her sister, Emma tried to visualize Sophie engaging in such tactics. Maybe it hadn't been for any self-centered reason. Maybe it had only been because she wanted Emma to be happy, too.

Emma shook her head. Emma didn't know what would make her happy. What could make Sophie believe she knew?

Palms outstretched, Emma closed the cabinet door with a quiet click. Pushing up from the floor, she gave Sophie and the customer a wide berth while making her way to the counter to look for the price tags. She glanced at her sister as she passed by her, noting the way she stood with arms down but crossed at the wrist, fingers interlocked, body leaning slightly forward. She looked politely but sincerely interested in whatever the customer was saying. She'd always possessed that demeanor. It served her well, but it wasn't false. This was Sophie, through and through. Perhaps Emma needed to pay closer attention and learn something. According to human resources at her exit interview, Emma rubbed people the wrong way.

She hadn't always though. She knew she hadn't. At what point in her life had she changed?

As if sensing Emma's gaze, Sophie turned her head and smiled, a brief, gentle smile that nevertheless shot like an arrow straight and rather painfully into Emma's heart. "I…hang tags?" Emma whispered, pointing toward the blue-tiled countertop.

"Bottom drawer left," Sophie told her before returning to her conversation with the man standing nearby.

"Bottom drawer left, bottom drawer left," Emma chanted under her breath. At the counter she squatted and yanked the indicated drawer open. Although not tidy, the drawer did hold a tag-filled sandwich bag as well as multiple ballpoint pens. Emma decided on the purple one. Having freed the two items from the jumble, she started to rise. A photograph fluttered to the ground. With a gasp, Emma seized it.

Jack. Jack and Emma and Sophie as teenagers, sprawled out on the Adirondack chairs on the porch, grinning at the camera. Eyes narrowed, she studied Jack's easy posture, his broad smile, the unkempt condition of his clothes and hair—it looked like he had just returned from a foray into the fields. He often did that, searching the field boundaries for interesting oddments turned up by the plow, unearthing old glass bottles and fragments of who-knew-what. Sure, there stood a bottle balanced on Jack's knee, a lovely sea green color with the added bonus of a half-rotted cork still in place.

While Sophie remained distracted, Emma rummaged further through the drawer, discovering tucked up against the edge an envelope filled with photographs. She flicked through them. They were all centered in and about their old home and contained not only Sophie and Emma, but all family members. The photos naturally included friends as well. Most conspicuously, Jack. She and Jack had been inseparable for so very long, friends first, and much more than that later.

A weight dropped into Emma's stomach. She shoved the loose photo in with the others and pushed the drawer shut. Unable to imagine why Sophie had all those family photographs stuffed into the drawer, Emma rose. Knowing Sophie, she'd been reliving old memories now that she'd returned home, but it seemed odd to be doing it in the store. Whatever the reason, Emma had no plans to ask. She wouldn't open up that floodgate. She wanted no strolls down memory lane, as the saying went. No revival of days gone by. Emma especially didn't want to talk about Jack. Talking about Jack would lead to Emma confessing what she'd learned, which would in turn encourage Sophie and her belief in fate. After all, both Emma and Jack had returned to Connor Falls at the same time, blah, blah, blah.

Sophie had finished with her customer, who was leaving the store with a promise to return. Sophie watched him until he'd disappeared through the door, and then she spun to face Emma. Starting guiltily, Emma clutched the sandwich bag filled with tags to her chest.

"What's going on, Ems?" Sophie asked.

"What do you mean?" In Emma's whirling thoughts, the question could pertain to many things. Emma dumped the tags onto the counter, beginning to untangle the thin threads, avoiding her sister's eye.

When Sophie didn't answer, Emma said, "If you're asking why I've changed my mind about selling some of my stuff in your store, well, why not? That jewelry isn't doing me any good lying in a box in my trunk. And I…I was touched that you thought of me, Soph. It took me a sleepless night to get my head around all of that. Sorry for my usual delay."

"And?"

Emma shot a glance at Sophie's earnest expression before returning to struggling with the fine threads. "And what?"

"Do you think you'll give Will English a call?"

Emma shrugged. "Probably. Not right this second, though. I'm in the middle of something." Goodness, she sounded like a petulant child. All she wanted, though, was not to be hounded, not to be the subject of implied fantasies about her returning to Connor Falls, not to be expected to make decisions about her life immediately. She'd given herself a timeframe. She'd stick to it. She'd promised herself she would. "Let's get through Christmas, first, shall we?"

"Sure," said Sophie in a flat tone. "Let's get through Christmas." She grabbed some knotted tags from the counter and began to assist in pulling them apart, keeping her gaze firmly glued to the task.

Emma studied her sister from the corner of her

eye. Sophie's fingers moved listlessly in an attempt to detangle the tag threads and eventually stopped. She dropped her hands to her sides, pushed her palms along her thighs. Her head lifted, looking past Emma to the display shelves behind, although Emma suspected she wasn't looking at a single thing on them. Sophie's feelings were hurt, Emma knew. Emma regretted being the perpetrator, but she wasn't sure which had offended Sophie more, the fact she hadn't jumped on the phone to Hannah's buyer or her abrupt, verbal dismissal of Christmas as a calendar date to be gotten through rather than what Sophie viewed as a season.

Sophie had always loved Christmas. That Sophie had invited Emma to spend it with her meant something special to Sophie. It wasn't casual to her. It was joyful and spiritual and nostalgic and magic. Kind of like Sophie's shop, Emma realized, straightening from the hopelessly tangled tags for a look around.

Why hadn't she noticed straightaway? This shop reflected Sophie more deeply than Emma had understood. It celebrated what her sister believed in, the wonder she held in her heart. No surprise people loved it. No surprise people loved her.

"I'm a river, Soph," Emma stated quietly, "with no calm place. You, you're a small and shimmering lake."

*　　*　　*

A *lake?* Sophie stood a moment, struck speechless by her sister's statement. Where the heck had that come from? A bland and boring lake, while Emma imagined herself as something roaring and powerful and never-ceasing. Huh. Maybe not quite that, but essentially the comparison was there.

"Well thanks," Sophie said, returning to her struggle with the hang tags.

"I think you misunderstood me," said Emma. "What I mean is you have depth and you're serene and comforting to be around. I run fast and shallow, can end up all over the place and give no one comfort, I'm afraid."

Sophie's cheek twitched. After a moment, she laughed and tossed the tags down onto the tile counter. "In that case, those were two rather amazing metaphors. Maybe you should take up writing in your spare time. However, you're none of those things, Ems. What would make you say so?"

"Because that's the way I feel."

"Oh, goodness," said Sophie. "I'm so sorry. I don't...I don't know what to say, except it isn't true. You're not a river. I don't think of rivers like that, anyway."

Emma jerked her head in a short nod. She wanted to drop it, Sophie could tell. The bell jangled at the front door. Glancing back, Sophie spotted a woman moving straight to the desk and chair set Mrs. Rood had pointed out. "I—I'll be right back."

"Okay," said Emma, giving the tags a tug. Several broke free, the threads still remarkably intact. Sophie headed across the store.

"Hi, I'm Sophie," she said to the woman standing with her chin in her hand, studying the desk. "If you have any questions, I'll be at the counter and happy to answer them."

"Thank you," the woman responded absently, taking a turn around the set. She lifted the price tag and released it as Sophie walked away. This was a customer who didn't want to be bothered. If the woman needed to know more, she'd come looking.

In the thirty seconds Sophie was gone, Emma had disappeared. Sophie snapped her head from side to side. "Ems?" she called softly.

"Over here," Emma answered from somewhere near the floor. Sophie found her on her knees before the cabinet, tags and pen in her hand, listless focus on the objects inside. With an eye on the customer, Sophie bent close so only her sister could hear.

"What happened today, Emma? Something momentous, I'd say."

Emma breathed in and out, her sweater rising and falling. "I…" One syllable, nothing more, and her voice trailed off.

"Don't make me drag it out of you, sis," Sophie threatened with a gentle smile.

"I ran into Jack," Emma said.

"Where?" Sophie realized how loudly she'd asked the question when the customer turned around with raised eyebrows. Sophie lowered her voice again. "Seriously, Ems, where?"

"At Luke's Tree Farm. I stopped for a wreath for Mom and Dad but, as Jack pointed out, it wasn't likely to get there on time."

"Right," Sophie drawled. "So it wasn't a quick how-do-you-do."

"It wasn't a particularly long conversation either," said Emma quietly, "but it was significant."

Sophie was dying to know, but the woman up front lifted a hand to wave her over. "I'll be just a minute," Sophie said. "Don't go clamming up on me when I get back. I want to know what's got you so off balance."

It happened that Sophie spent longer than a minute with the customer, who now had many questions and finally ended up putting a deposit down on the set, promising to come back for it before week's end. Sophie pulled the desk and chair from the floor and placed them in the storeroom. By the time she returned, Emma was full bore into pricing and barely looked up when she approached.

Sophie stood over her, hands on her hips. "How's it going?"

"Fine," said Emma, although she sounded anything but. "I'm guessing on these prices. You'll let me know if I'm off-base, won't you?"

"Sure."

At her short response, Emma glanced up at her and away.

"So, you bumped into Jack," Sophie prompted

again, "and…?"

"And he wanted to have coffee."

Sophie knew that couldn't be all. No matter how emotional her state these past couple days, Emma wouldn't lose composure over an invite to a hot beverage. Even with Jack. "That was friendly," Sophie said, almost like a question.

"Yeah," said Emma, abruptly giving Sophie her full attention, her brown eyes wide. "And I ran away."

Sophie had a sudden, vivid image of her sister hightailing it like a rabbit. "Surely not…not literally?"

"Just about."

"No," said Sophie on a breath.

"Right after he told me he wasn't married anymore."

Stunned, Sophie's mouth dropped open. She covered her parted lips with her hand. "When did that happen?" she asked through her fingers.

"I told you. When I stopped at Luke's. Forty-five minutes ago, maybe?"

"I don't mean the conversation," Sophie said. "I mean Jack's marriage."

"Oh, right," said Emma. Turning away again,

she picked up several tags she hadn't used and twirled them between her fingertips, watching them spin. "I don't know. I didn't ask. I just took off."

Sophie almost blurted out that Jack still cared for Emma, but she held it back. The last thing Emma needed was to go searching for whatever strength she required right now in a man she'd once loved. Emma had to find that strength inside her, now more than ever.

"Maybe coffee wouldn't have been the best idea, then," Sophie said.

"He was offering as a friend, so we could talk. I'm thinking he needed a friend, too. I didn't even ask what had happened. For all I know, she might have died or something."

Sophie sighed, dismayed by Emma's quick assumptions, her easy guilt. "What were his exact words?"

"I'm not married anymore."

"Divorced, then," Sophie said. "A widower would have expressed it differently."

"Do you think I should have had coffee with him?"

Lifting a shoulder, Sophie backed away. "Not

my call, Ems. The only thing I'm thinking is that you can't straighten out your life by complicating it further, but you might find some peace of mind if you talk things through with him. That's your decision, though. But remember, I'm here for you, okay?"

"That sounds ominous," Emma said.

"Not meant to be. Only trying to be supportive."

Emma rose from the floor. She dusted off her knees, her expression suddenly determined. "You're right," she said.

Sophie raised both hands. "Whoa, I'm not taking responsibility for any decisions you make. They're yours. But I'll have your back, Ems, you know I will."

"No, seriously, you are right," Emma went on, ignoring her. "I gave myself a timeframe for getting my life back on track. I don't need complications, I need forward momentum. Even if I wanted to reach out to Jack, clear the air, I don't have his phone number, so I don't—what?"

Sophie could have cursed her oh-so-readable face. She closed her eyes, opened them again. From beneath a creased brow, Emma's attention was suddenly focused, intent, suspicious.

"Sophie. What?"

"I have his number," Sophie admitted reluctantly. "He gave it to me for you yesterday, when he was here."

Chapter Seven

Emma stood outside in the cold waiting for Jack to show up. She held the note with his phone number crumpled against her chest in her hand, like a talisman.

Time to face your past, Emma Parsons.

Time to stop being a coward.

Had she always been this way? Not that she could recall. She'd once considered herself a fierce presence in the human race, someone with smarts, someone to be reckoned with, who planned to take on the world. Not a coward. Never a coward.

Once more she opened the note between her fingertips, studying the well-remembered slant that had marked Jack's handwriting. He'd written down both his first and last name, as if she'd relegated him to the annals of ancient history, a distant profile without connection.

Had it been a natural inclination to do so, because he'd been thinking about her in that fashion? Or, perhaps he hadn't been thinking of her at all. He'd had a whole other life. And she'd needed one.

The door to the coffee shop opened. Emma stepped aside for a couple exiting into the chill air. Breath rose in wisps from their mouths, meeting the steam rising from covers on delicious-smelling brew. The afternoon sun had quickly moved toward the horizon and two days in northern climes hadn't gone very far in getting Emma used to the freezing temperatures. She eyed the patrons through the window, at least half with their coats draped across chair backs. Clearly, *they* were warm.

"Why on earth are you waiting outside?"

Emma spun on her heel toward Jack's voice. "I—

um…" She didn't want to speak the truth, which was that she stayed outside so she could make a hasty retreat if she changed her mind. She didn't want to say anything at all once she got a good look at him. Her heart rolled over.

"Hi," she said. Like an idiot.

Smiling crookedly, he leaned to the side and peered through the plate glass window. "Any tables left?" he asked.

"There might be one in the corner," Emma answered slowly.

"Nope, someone just sat down there."

Emma experienced a twinge of disappointment. "Oh. Well, why don't we—"

"Get a nice big one to go? That sounds good."

"You need a coffee that bad, do you?" Emma teased. She wanted to kick herself for falling into that kind of lighthearted repartee. "We can do that and reschedule, if you'd like."

He turned from his table assessment to give her the onceover. "Actually what I was thinking was that we'd both get a nice hot cup of coffee to hang onto and take a walk. Or have those Georgia winters thinned your blood to water? You are shivering a bit."

"It's cold," she said defensively, before she had a chance to register what he'd said. How did he know she'd been living in Georgia? Oh, right, Sophie had likely blurted it out when he'd stopped in the store.

Jack tapped on the window frame, where a thermometer hung. Incentive, Emma figured, for customers to flock inside. "It's forty-two degrees."

Emma narrowed her eyes at him.

After a moment he laughed and shrugged. "Just saying, Georgia-blood."

With his easy way, he acted like they hadn't spent years apart. Enough. Stepping past him, Emma grabbed the handle and yanked the door open. Jack followed her inside.

"My treat," he said.

"I'll have a plain old coffee, then, two sugars, two creams."

"Hasn't changed, eh?"

He remembered. Why? Why would he remember something so mundane? Jack Winters, she thought, you're scaring me.

Beside her in line at the counter, he chuckled. "Am I?"

Oh, crap, had she said that out loud? "I—" She stopped. She wasn't about to explain herself. It would only get worse if she did. Instead, she bit her lip and picked up a nearby glossy sheet from a shelf, turning it over in her hand. The slick paper announced something called The Garland Ball.

"Wow," said Jack, "they've reinstated that, have they?"

Grunting, Emma returned the paper to its place. She didn't want to discuss the quirky events Connor Falls might be planning. "I don't even remember it."

"You're really not happy to be home, are you?"

Emma bit her lip again. She released a long breath through her nose. "I don't know what I am," she said.

Jack studied her in silence before stepping forward to give their order. Emma backed away from the counter, allowing room for several more people who had entered after they had, and also to obtain some breathing space. She hadn't meant her meeting with Jack to go this way, off-balance and revealing and uncomfortable. In her head it had been more like a quasi-interview, skirting around personal feelings and dealing instead with facts.

"Here you go."

With a jerk back to the moment, Emma reached out for the to-go cup Jack held out. She circled her fingers around it, bringing the cup to her nose and breathing in the scented steam drifting through the slit on top.

"A table's opened up by the window, if you'd rather?" Jack said, tipping his head toward the huge expanse of glass.

"No," said Emma, surprising herself, "let's walk. What's a little frostbite, when the coffee's good, right?"

"It's forty-two degrees," Jack reminded her. "Frost bite isn't even in the forecast."

"If you say so," said Emma, pulling open the door and stepping out onto the sidewalk. She looked left and right. "Which way?"

"To the park?"

Emma glanced down at her feet. At least she'd had the sense to put on her winter boots. "To the park," she said, steeling herself to remain unemotional, to discuss specifics and not sentiment. She started off toward the park without the slightest need to think about direction, aghast that she recalled so clearly. She'd been determined for so long to put Connor Falls behind her and yet it had remained somewhere inside, like a virus.

Jack walked beside her, not speaking. She cut her gaze sideways several times, catching the look of him, the way he walked, the forward tilt of his head, dark hair brushing across his brow, and bit her lip again. She could do this, she could.

"So," Jack said after slurping still-too-hot coffee from his cup, face contorting in a quick flinch, "tell me what's wrong."

It took no more than that, a simple request from the well-remembered Jack, to destroy her determination. The words flowed from her mouth as if they'd been released from a faucet: the artistic stagnation in her job, the self-doubt, the withdrawal from her friends, the increased tension at work, the final blow-up, the destruction of the life she'd fashioned, the defeated return to Connor Falls.

When she finally stopped babbling, Emma realized they were deep in the park, which had been decorated for the holidays. Quaint and somewhat cheesy, the holiday figures lining the path, the stars hanging from the branches and the light-wrapped trees glimmering in the twilight, made her break into tears.

Jack didn't make a move to touch her. If he had, she would surely have run away and never, ever looked back. Instead, he stood an arm's length from her studying a caroler made from plywood and paint. He rocked a little on his heels, coffee in one hand, the other tucked into his coat pocket.

Eventually he pulled the hand out, holding up a tissue in his gloved fingers.

"Don't worry," he said, "it's clean."

Lips quivering on the verge of either more tears or laughter, Emma took the tissue and blew her nose.

"You came back to Connor Falls," Jack said once she'd completed the noisy process, "because you needed to be home."

"Connor Falls isn't—"

"It is, Ems," said Jack.

Emma opened her mouth to argue further, but closed it without speech. In the near distance, church bells sounded the hour. Five o'clock. No wonder it was very nearly dark, the lights glowing ever more brightly on the trees. Tipping her head back, Emma listened to the voices on the sidewalk and unseen on the park's pathways. She thought of Sophie, steady, maternal Sophie and her wonderful little shop. She considered the photos she'd found in the counter drawer. Memories came rushing back at her. And she didn't cringe from them. Not one little bit.

"It is," Jack said again.

Maybe he was right.

*   *   *

Sophie lowered the wrapped box into the bag's flat bottom and gave the bag handles a little shake to make sure it had settled properly. She slipped the already marked promotional postcard in next to the box. Now that she'd put the postcards on the counter, she actually remembered them every time.

"All set," Sophie said.

The woman who'd been hovering near the greeting card rack strolled back to the counter. "Your store was recommended to me by someone earlier today. Out at the tree farm," the woman said, scooping up the paper satchel. "I don't live around here, but I'm glad I came."

"I'm glad you did, too," said Sophie with a smile. "Was it Luke, the owner? I'll have to thank him."

"No, though I did meet him. It was someone else. He didn't work there, but he helped me tie the tree to my roof. Will…something." The woman shrugged. "He mentioned you by name. Maybe you'll figure out who it is."

"English?" Sophie asked. The name simply popped out. He was the only Will she knew.

"That's it," said the woman. "Nice man. Thank you for the gift wrap, it's lovely. And have a wonderful Christmas."

"You do the same," Sophie responded, pleased that Will English had mentioned her store. She was even more tickled he had remembered her name. He must really want Emma's jewelry for Hannah's.

Frigid air blasted through the store as the customer exited. Outside the crisp night had settled in. Sophie tilted her arm to read the watch face resting against her wrist. Her stomach growled. Emma had offered to make dinner and bring it down to the store for them to eat, but she hadn't yet returned from her coffee meet-up with Jack.

Ignoring the time and her grumbling digestive system, Sophie wondered how the meeting was going. Given Emma's recent state of mind, Sophie had a tough time imagining. The fact Emma hadn't yet returned could mean just about anything.

When her stomach growled again, Sophie dove toward the mini-refrigerator. Her leftover yogurt from earlier in the day would have to do for now.

She and little bump couldn't wait any longer.

The door opened. Sophie sighed, snagging the yogurt from the fridge. Every time she put something in her mouth lately, someone was catching her at it—probably because she was always eating. Hoping to find Emma with something like take-out in her arms, she scrambled upright.

Will English stood hunched in his coat about a half dozen feet from the closing door, his eyebrows arching. "Did I catch you at a bad time? That's not your dinner, is it?"

Sophie waved the yogurt cup. "No, I'm waiting on Emma for that, but it's getting late and I'm starving. Sorry if she hasn't called you yet. She's been running around a bit today."

"No rush," said Will, strolling further into the store. He picked up a candle, lifted the lid, sniffed, and then absently replaced it, returning the candle to the shelf. Shoveling in yogurt, Sophie waited. It appeared Will had something on his mind. Sophie really hoped he wasn't about to tell her Hannah's now carried candles.

"Oh," she said in sudden recollection, "thank you for sending a customer my way." When he looked confused, she added, "From the tree lot? She said you helped her tie her tree onto her car."

"Sorry, right. I remember." He picked up another candle but didn't open this one, rolling it instead between his hands.

Sophie set the yogurt container down and jabbed the spoon into what little remained at the bottom. "Um, did you…did you need help finding something or…"

Blowing a breath out his nose, Will turned to put the candle back where he'd found it. Unfortunately, he jostled it into two more and the three candles clanked together. With an exclamation, he hastened to amend the situation and knocked one right over. Trying not to laugh, Sophie hurried around the counter to his aid.

"I know they're glass, but the containers are made to withstand heat so they're not as fragile as one might think." She returned everything to its proper place. "No harm done."

"Thanks," he said.

"You're welcome. What's up? Are you all right?"

"Is it that obvious?"

"Well, yeah," said Sophie, jerking her head toward the candles with a smile.

He drew a deep breath, one she heard him suck right in, and released it. His lips twisted into a crooked grin. "Silly, that I should be so nervous about this. Makes a good impression, doesn't it?"

Sophie's brow creased. "No worse than throwing the merchandise around," she joked in uncertain tones. Maybe she'd been totally wrong. Was he going to withdraw his offer to purchase Emma's designs?

"Well, I guess I should get right to it. It's just been a while and… What?"

A vague suspicion began to circle in Sophie's brain as he spoke. She had no idea what he could see in her face, but she managed to compose her expression. "Nothing," she said. "Go on."

"Okay. Good. Would you like to have dinner sometime?" he asked, running the words together. "With me," he added unnecessarily.

"I—I figured you meant with you," Sophie said, fighting the urge to giggle at the ridiculously endearing way he had asked. However, laughing right then, even something as tiny as a giggle, would probably chase him straight out the door.

"I guess this is unexpected."

"Yes," Sophie agreed, "it is unexpected. And rather complicated." She bit her lip.

"Ah, the store. Busy time for you. Not much time for dinner. How about something quick like a drink?"

"It's not that. It's—"

"Oh, you're involved. I asked, but I guess I was misinformed." He backed two steps away and paused, one eyebrow arched. "*Are* you involved with someone?"

Goodness, he was charmingly inept at this. He hadn't seemed that sort at all when he'd been in the store the first time. "I…no, it's—"

"Got it. I understand," he said, and took one more step.

"No," Sophie said, "you don't. I assure you, you don't. I'm pregnant, Will. Just pregnant."

*　　*　　*

Emma strode along the sidewalk, head bent against the cold, chin tucked into the bright red scarf tied around her neck. Every time she breathed, she smelled him in it, his aftershave's scent or his soap. Before they'd parted ways, Jack had wrapped his scarf around her neck. He called it a loaner, saying she could return it to him when she got her own. As if he expected to see her again. As if the absurdly intimate kindness wouldn't send her skittering away.

And it hadn't. She'd merely thanked him and told him she'd get the scarf back to him soon. As if she expected to see him again, too.

Hunching her shoulders, Emma burrowed her face a little deeper into the knit protection. She really didn't know that she would see him again. Making such a choice seemed like the rabbit hole she ought to avoid. But the spiral of her recent life appeared suddenly to have slowed. Maybe the spewing out to Jack regarding recent events had contained some catharsis in a way saying those same things to her sister hadn't. To be honest, she'd left out quite a bit in her breakdown to Sophie. Jack had heard it all.

Compared to most men she knew, Jack showed no inclination to fix it, to tell her what she should or shouldn't do. He was like Sophie that way. A good car.

A good man.

In which case, not like Sophie. Emma snorted into the scarf.

Spotting the Chandlery sign, Emma tightened her grip on the bag in her hand and quickened her pace. Despite her promise to make dinner, the sub sandwiches she'd picked up were going to have to do. Sophie had to be starving by now.

Only slightly touched by remorse at having been gone so long, Emma yanked open the shop door. Sophie stood about three feet from the counter staring at the floor. She didn't even look up when Emma entered.

"Soph?" Emma hurried forward. "You okay?"

With a start, Sophie looked around. "Hey, Ems."

"What's wrong?"

"I…"

Emma clutched Sophie's arm, giving it a little shake. "Are you feeling all right? Is the baby—"

"Baby's fine." Turning on her heel, Sophie's lips twisted up into a crooked, sheepish smile. "Sorry, didn't mean to scare you. I just…well…I have a date."

Emma's mouth dropped. "A date? Like, a *date* date?"

"Yes," Sophie said in a slow drawl, eyebrows arching, "like a date date."

"I don't—"

"I know."

"But I—"

"Yep."

"With who?" Emma finally managed.

Sophie's lip quirked up again. "Well, aye, there's the rub. With Will English. Your possible new employer or whatever he would be called. And before you ask, no, I didn't agree to go out with him to make sure he takes your jewelry."

"That last part was a pretty lousy attempt at a joke, Soph. But does he—" Emma's eyes flicked toward Sophie's stomach and back up. "Does he know?"

"Of course," Sophie said, turning and walking behind the counter. "I told him straight out. How could I not, especially if we sat down to dinner and he found himself paying for three? I eat like a horse these days. Seriously though," she added, searching across the tiled countertop for something she didn't seem focused enough to find, "whatever he expects from a date or two, I certainly didn't want to find myself in a position of telling him later. He'd think I'd been holding back some deep, dark secret. And there's nothing secret about the fact I'm having a baby and certainly nothing dark."

"I agree," Emma said, although a small part of her had been wondering what Sophie planned to do about letting people know. Obviously, this was what she would do. Straight and open Sophie Parsons all the way. "How'd he react?"

Sophie shrugged. "Okay. I think. He still wants to go out. Hot chocolate and fresh baked goods from Gina's, then a stroll to listen to the carolers in the park."

"Good Lord," said Emma, "he sounds perfect for you."

A little burst of air slipped from Sophie's nose as she smiled. "Would you mind watching the store for me tonight? Only for a little while near closing. You can call me if you have any problems."

"I'd love to."

"Liar."

"Well, I'll do it, no matter how great my fear of the cash register. And customers. And questions,"

Emma said with a laugh.

"Thank you, Ems."

"You're welcome, Sophie." They stared at each other for longer than usual. A tiny chill danced down Emma's spine, followed by rushing warmth. Emma wanted to run across the store and take her sister into her arms in a great, big hug. Instead, she reached up to slip Jack's scarf from around her coat collar.

"You broke down and bought yourself a scarf?" Sophie nodded at the garment now in Emma's grip.

Emma's fingers tightened around the weave, squeezing out cold air. "It's Jack's. He loaned it to me."

Sophie's hand hovered above the small tray where she kept paper clips beside the register. With a quick movement she snatched out a purple clip and fastened together two sheets of paper from the counter. "Jack's, huh?"

"Yes," said Emma. "Jack's."

"And he loaned it to you."

"Yes."

"So he expects to see you again to get it back."

"I—yes."

Sophie's lips curved. She started humming "It's

Beginning to Look a Lot like Christmas" as she gathered up several more papers and clipped them together, too.

"What?" demanded Emma, starting to feel like she was being judged.

"I didn't say anything. Are there sandwiches in that bag? I'm starving."

Emma marched to the counter and dumped the bag's contents across it. "The turkey is yours. I'm assuming you're still okay with turkey? No odd non-cravings?"

Bringing the wrapped sandwich to her nose, Sophie breathed the contents in deeply. "Turkey's not one of them." She ripped off the paper and took a huge bite from the end, talking around it. "Your time with Jack went well, then?"

"You could say that." Emma carefully pulled the tape from the wrapping on her own sandwich.

"Well I sort of just did." Sophie paused eating long enough to twist the cap from a water bottle and take a swig. "I'm asking what you thought of it."

Emma considered for a long time. She ate half her sandwich while Sophie quietly consumed hers, waiting, remaining more patient than Emma could believe. Sophie had started in on a dark chocolate bar stuffed with caramel Emma had hoped they'd share later before Emma opened her mouth and answered.

"He's still Jack," she said.

Sophie bit her lip.

"He's still *my* Jack," Emma amended.

Sophie gathered her trash, crumpled it and dropped it into the can beneath the counter. "Literally or figuratively?"

Emma thought about that. While she and Jack talked, the years apart had been glaringly evident, but she'd realized they'd only been so because in an organic and natural way they had disappeared, vanishing not as if they'd never existed, but as if they didn't really matter. She'd relaxed into herself for the first time in ever so long. As for Jack, the expression in his eyes when he looked at her had torn her heart to shreds in a lovely, delicious and frightening way. Jack, her Jack…still.

She bowed her head, fingering the red scarf stuffed into her pocket. "It could be both," she whispered, "and I don't know what to do."

"Well, you'd best figure it out, sis," Sophie said, coming around the counter to do exactly what

Emma had decided to forgo, wrapping her arms around Emma and squeezing her tight. "Time marches on whether we keep up with the beat or not."

Chapter Eight

Sophie, as usual, was absolutely right. Not that Emma could figure out her whole life in the next few days, but she ought to be able to figure out a part of it, if only a tiny little part of it.

Like what to do what all her mixed-up emotions regarding Jack, emotions that had been hanging on since…well, since the day they broke up. Not really a tiny part at all.

In frustration, Emma banged the side of her head lightly against the door's edge. She returned her focus to Sophie and Will English strolling side by side along the sidewalk, heading for the bakery and then the park on their simple, but perfect, first date. When they reached the corner Emma stepped back inside, pulling the door shut. She wrapped her arms around herself against the cold she'd let in, thoughts shooting guiltily to Sophie's heating bill.

Will appeared to be a nice man. His interest in Sophie was obvious, in his smile, his quiet solicitation, the corny jokes he made three times in ten minutes to make her feel at ease. He needn't have bothered with the latter. Sophie seemed quite comfortable in his company—maybe too comfortable. Did she not have the same interest in him?

Emma dismissed that idea as quickly as it came to her. Sophie had always been confident, calm, something that had intimidated the boys back in high school who expected someone giddy and flustered and perhaps a little in awe of them. Emma had envied Sophie's self-assurance.

Going over in her mind the steps Sophie had shown her for using the register—why was she so nervous about this?—Emma returned to the counter and took up a place behind it. She ran her fingers over the smooth, lovely blue surface Sophie had created before sticking her hands in her back pockets. Only an hour or so and Sophie would be back to close up the store.

When some time passed without a customer, Emma figured they must all be at the park observing the caroling. Her shoulders relaxed. Remembering the photos by her feet, Emma bent and opened the drawer. She had a sudden, stupidly sentimental desire to view the old photographs again. Except for the pens, the tag-filled bag and two or three post-it notes, the drawer was empty.

"Crap," Emma muttered. She pushed the drawer shut, holding her hand flat against it. Really, she didn't need to get caught up in reminiscence. All she needed was to get her head on straight.

Even as she tried to dismiss her curiosity, Emma pulled open the other drawers. Rummaging through each one, she didn't find a single photo. Wondering what Sophie had done with them all, Emma searched several baskets on the shelf. One held the promotional postcards and another held a stack of invoices. The last contained only a pad filled with handwritten notes. She glanced at the top page, which resembled an informal holiday inventory.

As the store remained empty, Emma decided to take a quick peek in the storage room. On the long worktable, evidence of Sophie's craft was everywhere. Emma located more notes pinned to a huge corkboard, these scribbled with new scent ingredients and sketched designs for a painting on a child's desk. At the bulletin board's far end a single photo hung, too large to be what Emma had been searching for. She sidled over for a look anyway.

Sophie had blown up a photo she'd taken of herself holding a sonogram picture angled beside her cheek. Across the bottom she had written the words, "This is us."

This is us.

Emma's breath rushed out in unexpected response to the scrawled sentiment. She pressed her fingers to her mouth. Tears ran down her cheeks. She missed Sophie, missed the rest of the family, she even missed this town, for crying out loud. What on earth was wrong with her, getting all emotional? Besides the wreck of her life, of course—that could explain something, but not quite all. Christmas blues? Maybe. Jack? Definitely.

Emma hurried from the storeroom, scrubbing her damp eyes with fists clenched like a child's. "Get a grip," she muttered fiercely.

"Are you all right?"

Emma's hands dropped. Her eyes flew wide. "Jack! I didn't even hear the door open!" In her shock, she sounded as though she were accusing him of sneaking in. "I'm sorry. I—"

"The door wasn't quite closed. The bell didn't ring," Jack said, jerking a thumb over his shoulder toward the offending entryway. His brown eyes studied her in frowning concern. "What's happened, Ems? Are you okay?"

"It's nothing. Everything is fine."

His expression changed in a way she couldn't quite read.

"Really," she insisted, even though she had to give her right cheek another swipe. "It is."

Jack let loose a long, deep sigh and shook his head. "Emma, you haven't changed. You fight the fight alone, even though there are people who care about you, who are willing to help or even just to listen. There always were."

"I know," Emma said quietly.

"Do you?"

"Of course I do."

Jack's lip twitched at the corner. He nodded toward the counter. "Where's your sister?"

"Sophie's out. On a date."

"A date?"

It did seem a bit absurd, when Emma thought about it. The last weekday evening prior to Christmas and Sophie goes out on a date, leaving her business in Emma's dubious control. Generally, though, Sophie wasn't irresponsible. She must possess some belief in Emma to do all the necessary things. Emma glanced quickly around the store before returning her attention to Jack. "What…what are you doing here, anyway?"

"Me?" said Jack. "I brought you something."

"You did?"

"I did."

"Coffee?"

"Not coffee." Jack reached into his jacket pocket and pulled out a small bundle wrapped in white tissue paper, tied around with a thin silver ribbon. He held the package out to her.

Emma raised her brows at the gift and hesitated. "What is it?"

Snatching her hand from her side, he dropped the package into her palm. "You're supposed to open it," he said. "That's how you find out."

Biting her lip, Emma tugged at the ribbon, releasing the bow. No tape had been used and the tissue paper fell away. Nestled inside lay a scarf in the loveliest green color Emma had ever seen, a color like springtime layered in fog. She lifted the scarf from the paper and held the soft weave to her cheek. "It's beautiful," she whispered.

Jack leaned forward on his toes, shoving both hands into his jeans pockets. "I figured if you're going to stick around a bit, you'll need your own."

"What makes you think I'm going to—" Emma began, and stopped. Jack's expression had softened, becoming almost amused and with something else lurking in his eyes, something that made Emma's heart leap in her chest.

"You might," he said. "It wouldn't hurt."

"Jack, I…" She couldn't say it, couldn't put into words all the turmoil, the longing, the confusion and indecision circling in her heart.

The hope.

"I know," he said. "Me, too."

*   *   *

Sophie sipped the hot chocolate in her hand. The past hour had been fun, so much fun, but now Will stood beside her in silence. The carolers were in rare form, yet she knew it wasn't only their talent suddenly tying his tongue.

They had been getting on, as her grandmother used to say, like a house a-fire. Sophie wasn't exactly sure what that meant, although it likely had something to do with the conflagration aspect. Yep, a house-afire, until…

Until.

Sophie lifted her head, shaking away the hair pressed into her eyes by her hat. She drank a little more hot chocolate.

He'd said her being pregnant didn't matter. They were going on a date, nothing else, just something fun to do together. But after a particularly long bout of laughter, or perhaps a smile held too long, she had witnessed the realization bloom in his eyes.

She was a package deal. If it came to that, anything he might hope for in the future included another little person.

Her gloved hand strayed to her coat front and rested there. Fa-la-las filled the air, nearly overpowering the church bells in the distance. Two teenage girls, twins from their nearly identical features and hair and bright pink hats, paused on the pathway, blocking Sophie and Will's view. Will stepped right, Sophie left, increasing the distance between what had been their bumping elbows. Sophie drank again, swallowing hot cocoa gone lukewarm.

Dating while pregnant had been the last thing on her mind. Dating during the busy Christmas season should have been. When she envisioned such a thing as a date—which came to her only in vulnerable moments few and far between—it had been as some vague consideration in the very distant future. She couldn't imagine what it would be like for Will or any man to embark on a path, however casual, with a woman carrying another man's child. Pending changes in enormous proportion had to float between them like a growing balloon they both knew would pop.

Still, Will had insisted even after she told him. Probably hadn't had enough time to process the facts. Or he was merely too nice to do an abrupt about-face.

Spotting a trash can, Sophie walked over and tossed the almost empty cup inside. She took off her gloves and stood a moment readjusting her scarf before pulling them back on. Her breath frosted in the air.

"Hey."

Sophie spun slowly on her heel. "Is for horses, my grandmother used to say."

"Mine, too," Will admitted. "I looked around and

you were gone.”

“Sorry about that. I was throwing away the dregs of my chocolate.”

Will reached past her, tossing his coffee cup in after hers. “The carolers are wonderful.”

“Amazing,” agreed Sophie.

“And so are you.”

Sophie’s shoulders jerked. “What?”

Will locked his gaze on hers, speaking quickly. “You’ve done a lot in the past couple of years. You were certain what you wanted and focused on getting there. You successfully accomplished many changes in your life. I’m sure having a baby wasn’t in the plans, and yet, well, you’ve made adjustments and you’re happy with them. I admire you.”

“Um, thank you.” Though pleased by his praise, Sophie sensed the “but” coming like a breath that could only be held for so long.

He turned toward the carolers as they began their next tune. “I just had to get that off my chest.”

Sophie moved up next to him. She pressed both hands deep into her coat pockets. “Because?”

He glanced at her and back to the singers. “I wanted you to know.”

“Because?” Sophie prompted again.

"Because," he said without looking at her, "I like you and—"

"And this is weird," Sophie finished for him.

He sighed in a swirl of white. "Not the word I would have used, but yes. This is weird."

There, out in the open now. Sophie lifted her chin, her gaze on the group performing before them. "I get it," she said. "I understand."

"Is it weird for you, too?"

Sophie thought for a second. "As an in-the-moment sort of thing, it was fine."

"Until you realized how well we were getting along," he said. "I'm asking myself, when has that ever been a bad thing?"

Sophie flinched, even though she knew he hadn't meant what he'd said in the way it sounded. "Getting along with another person is never a bad thing, Will. Sometimes, though, it can be complicated." Look at Emma and Jack, she thought, or even she and Emma, for crying out loud. Drawing a deep breath, she faced Will. "But I think we're getting ahead of ourselves."

He had raised his hands to clap along with everyone else at the song's conclusion, but slowly lowered them back to his sides. "Right," he said. "First date."

"First date," she echoed. She forced a crooked

smile to her lips. She didn't feel much like smiling. Odd. She'd been told she always had a smile for everything and everyone. "I really did have a wonderful time. This was pretty perfect for me, hot chocolate, a warm pastry, carols in the park, but I'm thinking I should get back to the store. Emma's not very experienced when it comes to handling customers."

Will's shoulders slumped inside his jacket, whether in relief or disappointment Sophie couldn't be sure. It might have been both. "Tell her I'll be giving her a call to schedule an appointment to meet," he said.

"I will." Sophie took a step back. She waited a second to see if he planned to offer to walk her to the store. His remark regarding a call to Emma seemed to indicate he wouldn't. "Enjoy the music," she said, to completely let him off the hook.

"Oh, no, I can—"

"I'm good," Sophie said. "You shouldn't miss the rest of the program." With another hard-won smile, she took a few more steps away from him and waved. Pivoting on her boot heel, she strode to the park entrance. She didn't trouble herself with listening for footsteps following after her. She knew there wouldn't be any.

*　　*　　*

Emma plugged in her phone and set it down quietly on the bedside table. She'd put it on silent an hour ago so as not to disturb Sophie. When the screen lit up yet again, Emma quickly read the text and typed a response before snuggling down into her pillow with a smile. She pulled the quilted blanket up to her chin, turning her gaze to the streetlight's glow outside the window.

Passing voices drifted like whispers through the glass and from the television in Sophie's bedroom. Sophie had claimed to be tired, exhausted from her day. Even so, Emma had begged for particulars about her date with Will English. Sophie had been non-communicative except to say it had been nice. Nice. What did that mean? When Emma briefly showed her sister the gorgeous scarf from Jack, Sophie hadn't had much to say about that either. She'd smiled, genuinely pleased, without asking any questions. None.

Something was off with her.

Emma picked up the phone to check the time. Nine-fifty-five: way too early for bed, especially considering all the thoughts zipping through her skull.

Emma listened for a few more minutes to the television. It had been on the same nearly non-existent volume since Sophie had said good night and slipped inside, quietly shutting the door behind. Trying to make as little noise as possible, Emma sat up, untangled her legs from beneath the covers and planted her feet on the floor. She hastened back into the clothes she'd removed a short time ago, pressing her feet into her winter boots. After wrapping the scarf from Jack around her throat, she snatched up her coat, her phone, her gloves and the key Sophie had given her to the back door, the one that led to the fire escape.

Stepping into the hallway, she heard nothing but the droning television from her sister's room. Emma crept closer and tipped her head toward the door. Slowly she turned the knob and peeked inside. "Oh," she said in surprise, "hi. I thought you were asleep."

The flickering light from the television screen danced over Sophie's face. "Just thinking. Where are you off to?"

"I'm not very tired. I thought I'd go for a walk."

Sophie whipped the covers back. "Want some company?"

"I—now? Sure. Okay."

Leaning against the doorjamb, Emma waited while Sophie hastily pulled clothes on over her sleep pants and tee shirt. At one point Sophie glanced in Emma's direction. "Lovely scarf," she said. "In case I forgot to say that earlier. From Jack?"

Emma grunted acknowledgement. Boy, Sophie's mind really must have been elsewhere. "He said I would need it if I decided to stick around a while."

"Nice man, our Jack."

Emma's lips curled.

"And are you?" Sophie asked, tugging on her boots. "Sticking around a while, I mean."

"Maybe."

Sophie paused in tying her bootlaces and then resumed the action, forming the bow with a quick snap. She straightened, fluffing her hair free from her sweatshirt collar. "Let's go to the pub. I'm not drinking, of course, but I could eat a horse."

"You're still hungry?"

With a smirk, Sophie aimed the pointer finger on both hands toward her stomach. Emma laughed and tossed Sophie's coat to her. She nodded toward Sophie's haphazard attire. "You don't want to put on something different?"

"Nope."

Together they clambered, giggling, down the

metal stairs outside. Low clouds overhead diffused light from the town's streetlamps. Snowflakes began to fall before she and Sophie had exited the alley.

Sophie lifted her face to the sky. "You okay with this?"

Emma pulled her scarf tighter around her throat and yanked up her hood. "Perfectly."

Snowflakes drifted onto their faces, shoulders, caught in their hair as Emma kept pace with her sister's stride. On the rare occasion they had snow in Georgia Emma stayed home. The feather-light sensation against her skin was something she hadn't realized she missed before this moment.

Abruptly, she halted to peer into a shop window.

"What?" Sophie returned to look around her outstretched arm.

"Those dresses are gorgeous," Emma whispered.

"You're smudging Cindy's window," teased Sophie. "Come on."

"Cindy? Not Cindy Michaels?" Emma and Cindy's younger sister had been in the same class. Cindy had made a marvelous blouse Emma had bought from her when she was a high school freshman.

Sophie nodded. "Yep."

"What a lovely store." Emma's brow wrinkled. "Maybe Cindy would be interested in a line of jewelry specifically designed to go with her dresses?"

"So," said Sophie quietly, "are you staying around a while, then?"

Emma backed from the window. She looked up and down the street, hard edges gentling in the snow. Sure, Connor Falls presented an enticing picture in all its Christmas finery, especially with a timely snowfall, but was it home?

It had been, once. Being here, now, with Sophie, made her remember that. She'd spent her adult years without roots. Standing in this town, on this sidewalk where she'd walked more times than she could possibly remember, she felt them stretching down below her feet and outward in every direction.

"Maybe," she said, wavering, because there was Jack. There would always be Jack.

Sophie studied her a long minute before tugging her sleeve. "Hungry. Me. Can you *not* hear my stomach growling?"

"Loud and clear, sis." Emma linked her arm through Sophie's and started once more toward the pub. At the corner, she stopped again. Her breath swirled through the snow. The tavern was close enough for voices and music to drift out through the opening door and become muffled when it shut. Emma met Sophie's gaze and held it.

"Does it ever feel like defeat?" she asked. "Coming back?"

Sophie smiled. "Not to me, Ems. Not ever."

Chapter Nine

Sophie stretched, squinting at sunlight glistening off the snow outside onto the ceiling above her bed. What a strange, exhilarating night she and Emma had wandered into at the pub, filled with noise and laughter and an exuberant, contagious cheerfulness. It wasn't the drink—well, for some perhaps it was the drink—it was more the atmosphere, the knowledge that these were the people she knew, and if she didn't know them, they still shared this town with her, and they were together celebrating the holiday season. Even Jack had been there, dining with some friends at a corner table. As soon as he spotted Emma he'd called out, "Georgia-blood!" and came to her side as if he'd never been away from it. They'd resolved something between them, those two. Sophie couldn't imagine when. There really didn't seem to have been enough time. Maybe there didn't need to be.

Exhausted from the late night, she'd wandered through yesterday bleary-eyed and stupefied, but fortunately Emma had been in attendance all day to lend a hand. Today though…today was Christmas.

Snuggling back beneath the covers, Sophie closed her eyes, palm resting flat on her abdomen. Last Christmas, the first with the Chandlery, she'd spent by herself. This Christmas she had Emma, and even if she hadn't, she still wouldn't have been alone. She could feel precious life within her like her own breath.

Suddenly, bare feet slapped along the hallway. Sophie heard the melodic beeping alerting Emma to a text on her phone. This was followed by two more. "Ems!" Sophie called lazily, "who's blowing up your phone?"

The door opened. Emma's tousled head appeared.

"Nobody. Go back to sleep. You need it."

"Jack?" Sophie persisted, grinning.

Emma shut the door.

"Fine," Sophie mumbled, "don't share." She rolled over, burrowing her cheek against the pillow. Peering through one eye, she brought the numbers on the nightstand clock into focus. She could afford another half hour. She'd put all the packages under the tree last night, including those she still had to mail, with apologies, to family. Their appearance around the Christmas tree made the living room look more festive. However, if she heard one crinkle of paper she'd be out there in a flash.

Remembering how Emma hated to wait, she yelled out to her as she passed by again. "No peeking!"

"I know," said Emma from the hall.

Satisfied, Sophie curled her fingers over the growing mound of her stomach. "Merry Christmas, little one," she whispered, closing her eyes.

When she next opened them it was exactly an hour and thirty-five minutes later and the apartment smelled like coffee and cinnamon. Sophie scrambled from the bed and into her robe and reindeer slippers. She hurried to the kitchen, where she found Emma tending to scrambled eggs in the frying pan. On the counter stood a platter filled from side to side with freshly baked cinnamon buns. Emma glanced over her shoulder.

"I was just getting ready to call you," she said. "Brunch is almost ready."

Sophie shuffled over to the buns and stuck her chin out over them, breathing in. "Did you make these from scratch?"

Emma snorted. "Remember who you're talking to, Soph."

"Right." Sophie scooped a bun from the plate and bit into it, icing dribbling onto her chin. Emma deftly flipped eggs onto plates, tucked toast at the edge and a bun for good measure. Beyond her, in the living room, two tray tables had been set up with utensils, napkins and steaming mugs.

Following her gaze, Emma said, "Yours is hot chocolate. Coffee for me, though, nice and strong."

"Remind me to keep you around."

"I don't think you have a choice," Emma shot back, carrying the plates into the living room.

Grinning, Sophie trailed after her sister. "Ems! You've been moving the gifts."

"Especially those," Emma said, pointing to four identical tubes. She sat at the table with her coffee and began eating. "I shook them a few times. Still can't figure it out."

"Well, open yours then," Sophie said, tucking into the eggs while they were still warm.

"Now?"

"Yes, now. I wish they'd been finished in time for me to mail the others out for Christmas, but at least you'll have yours."

Emma leaned sideways, stretching her whole body in order to grab the package with her name on the tag and not get up from her seat. Sophie had always removed the wrapping from her gifts with precision, saving the paper for craft projects. Emma, on the other hand, was a ripper. Paper littered the floor before Sophie had swallowed her second mouthful. Unrolling the tube's contents, Emma gasped. She tipped the printed collage toward the light streaming in through the window, exclaiming over each picture.

"I wondered what you were doing with all those photos in the drawer," she said. "You had one made for each of us?"

Sophie took another bite from the cinnamon bun in her left hand and nodded, warmed by Emma's smiles. "I reckoned the holidays we couldn't be together," she said around a mouthful, "we'd still have these reminders of ourselves as a family.”

Emma’s smile faded. “We’ll always be a family, Soph. Always.” Her phone vibrated on the table. She snatched it up for a quick read, pecked in a reply and put the phone down again before rising. “I’ve got something special for you, too.”

“Finish eating first,” Sophie said. “I have patience.”

“Well I don’t.” Emma headed for the back door, grabbing her coat and keys from a kitchen chair. “It was too big to fit under the tree. I’ll be right back.”

Sophie took her plate over to the window, watching for Emma on the sidewalk below. In the next few weeks or months, they would surely get under each other’s feet in this small apartment, but they’d adjust. Emma’s life was going to change, as would hers yet again in short order. It would be okay, though. Everything would work out as it should.

After a few minutes, Sophie realized Emma hadn’t exited the alley. She maneuvered around the tree for a better look, not finding her. At clanging footsteps on the fire escape, Sophie hurried back across the apartment in time to see a huge box with a bright red bow press against the glass in the door. Sophie swung the door open and stepped out of the way.

"Emma, what on earth have you done?" Sophie cried with a laugh. "Whatever's in that box is going to have to hang from the ceiling, because there sure as heck isn't any room on the—"

Sophie's hands flew to her mouth. On the fire escape landing behind Emma and the lowering and obviously empty box stood their brother Robbie and his wife with their two kids, while below them, waving and grinning, were Judy and her family.

"Merry Christmas, Soph," said Emma. "I knew this was what you wanted most of all."

*   *   *

Emma couldn't believe she'd pulled it off. Yet here they all were, together for Christmas, except Mom and Dad, of course. It had been impossible for them to get flights. Emma had made the calls early on Christmas Eve morning, never expecting anyone to change their plans. Well, how wonderfully nice to be so very wrong.

Her phone went off in her pocket. Emma pulled it out, smiling at the screen. This time the text was Jack, wishing her a merry Christmas. Where they were headed, she and Jack, Emma had no idea. She wouldn't count on anything, but she also wouldn't count anything out.

Leaning against the kitchen counter, Emma texted Jack back and returned the phone to her sweatshirt pocket. Robbie came into the kitchen with a load of dishes, depositing them in the sink. Everyone had brought something. There had been plenty to eat.

He kissed her on the cheek. "You've done good, sis," he said. With a grin, he shambled back into the living room.

She had, she had done good and doing good felt great.

Movement at the door caught her eye. A man stood centered in the window, looking over his shoulder. When he turned front, Emma recognized him straightaway. She hurried over to the door and opened it.

"Will?"

Stepping inside, Will glanced toward the living room. "Emma, hi. Merry Christmas. I…I actually didn't expect there to be a houseful today, from what Sophie had said. Can I…I'd like to talk to Sophie for a second."

"Sure." Catching Sophie's eye, Emma waved her

sister over and then vacated the area so they could speak. She tried not to look too many times in their direction, but as she wasn't the only one filled with curiosity, every eye eventually turned their way. One of June's children, Emma wasn't sure which, asked rather loudly, "Who's that with Aunt Soph?"

Laughing at the question, Sophie brought Will into the living room and introduced him.

"Will, you can stay for a bit, can't you?" Robbie asked. "Sit down. I'll get you a plate."

"I'll get it," Sophie said. She grabbed Emma's elbow on passing, tugging her into the kitchen. Emma held the empty plate Sophie handed her while Sophie ladled food onto it.

"What gives?" Emma asked. "Everything okay?"

Sophie arched a brow. "He said he can handle weird if I can."

Confused by the reference, Emma snorted. "And is that a good thing?"

Sophie took the dish from Emma's hands and smiled. "I guess we'll see."

As Sophie carried away the heaping plate, the phone in Emma's pocket sounded again. Emma yanked the phone out and read the message. *Would you have a little time to step outside?*

Rolling her eyes, she texted back: *Where are*

you? You are allowed to come up, you know.

I'm in front of the store. Let's take a quick walk.

Emma's gaze lifted to her family crammed into the living room. Except for Mom and Dad, they were all here, all together for the first time in quite a few years. An odd sensation crept into her chest, a mixture of heartache and incredible joy. For the first time, she thought she might truly understand why Christmas meant so much to Sophie—her little sister Sophie, soon to be a mom, standing to the side in observation and wearing a quiet and happy smile. As if sensing Emma's eyes on her, Sophie's turned in her direction. Emma pointed at the cell phone she held, then the door, and then made a silly walking motion toward it with her fingers.

Sophie's smile deepened. She nodded.

Emma grabbed her winter gear and went down through the store, to avoid a fuss. She wouldn't be long. By the time anyone noticed her absence she'd be back. After shutting and locking the shop door behind her, she stepped out into the frigid sunlight where Jack stood hunched in his coat, waiting for her.

"Nice scarf," he said.

"Yeah, some guy gave it to me. Apparently, he wanted his back."

"I'm sure that's not the only reason."

"I'm sure it isn't either," she said.

The slow spread into a grin she remembered so well hadn't changed at all. She didn't think it ever would. When she'd first bumped into Jack, she had worried those little reminders would always process as painful. She'd been wrong about so many things.

Jack tipped his head. "Walk?"

Emma fell in beside him, chilled hands stuffed into her pockets, chin tucked into the scarf's whisper-soft folds. Snow had fallen again during the night, freshly coating objects in a fluffy, crystalline layer. The cold bit at Emma's cheeks, but she had no urge to complain.

"Where are we going?"

"You tell me," he said.

"What?"

"Pick one place you really want to go within walking distance, and we'll go there."

Emma stopped dead on the corner. She could tell by Jack's expression he wasn't kidding. "I don't know of any," she said.

"Give it a minute, Ems. Some place will come to you."

Compressing her lips, Emma released a loud breath from her nose. "Okay," she said, "this way."

Turning left, she walked faster than she intended until she reached Connor Falls Book Emporium. Warmed by her pace, she halted before the front door. Jack strolled up slowly to a standstill beside her. Emma pressed near the glass, peering inside the closed, book-filled shop.

"I used to save up my babysitting money to come in here and buy books on jewelry-making," she said.

Jack nodded.

"You came with me once or twice," Emma added, meeting his eyes in their reflection. He'd sit beside her, patiently waiting while she viewed each page before deciding to buy. Drawing a deep breath, she headed back onto the sidewalk. "Am I only allowed one place?"

"Of course not," he said.

Checking for non-existent traffic, Emma trotted across the street, her rubber soles crunching the frozen slush piled near the curb. Outside From the Hart bakery, Emma eyed the gingerbread house front and center in the window. There'd been a bakery in this location since well before Emma's birth, most recently changing hands right before she went away to school.

"Gina still makes the best baked goods in Connor

Falls and beyond," Jack said beside her.

"Are you tricking me into a walk down Memory Lane?"

"Not tricking you at all, Ems. These choices are yours."

Right, she thought. Mine.

Walking more slowly, Emma continued down the block with Jack at her side, all the way to Hannah's. The huge building took up the whole corner, the first floor lined with enormous windows filled with Christmas displays in an amazing variety. There had always been something magical about Hannah's at Christmastime.

"The buyer for Hannah's is interested in my jewelry."

Jack said nothing, rocking a bit on his heels as he viewed their reflections in the glass. After a moment, Emma moved on, past the tavern where she and Jack and Sophie had had such fun two nights ago. When they reached the church, Emma clasped the black iron fence surrounding it in her gloved hands. The bells started up, beginning, as they always did at Christmas, with a few measures from a recognizable carol.

We talked about getting married here someday.

"We were young," Jack said, as if she'd said those words out loud. "Really young."

"I know."

"There's a lot of history, together and apart, and all of it is important, Ems. It makes us who we are now."

"I know," she said again.

He took a step sideways, closer, curling his hand over hers on the fence. "And then," he said in a quiet voice, "there's always the future."

"I know," she said, one last time. He leaned toward her, pressing his lips gently onto hers. The church bells filled the air with their old familiar song.

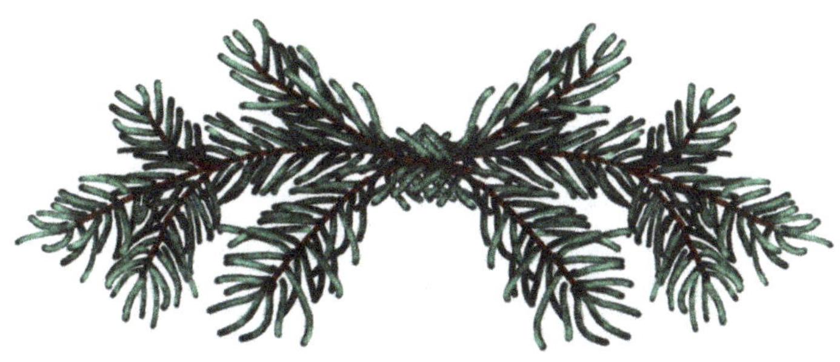

"I heard the bells on Christmas Day
Their old, familiar carols play,
And wild and sweet
The words repeat
Of peace on earth, good-will to men!"

Henry Wadsworth Longfellow